# THE Cozdle

## SHELBY CAMPBELL

## ACKNOWLEDGEMENTS

All thanks be to God for randomly inspiring me some four or five years after the completion of this book to finally put it out.

He really is full of surprises.

## TO THE READER

I wrote this book when I was sixteen and decided after months of preparation that it was not worth publishing. Now, fast forward to midnight on an uneventful day in June of 2017, when I was suddenly compelled to release it.

How…unexpected.

There are many things I could do now to make this piece better, edits I could spend time with to turn it into some sort of personal masterpiece. But then it would no longer be a representation of who I was as a writer four years ago.

I'm using this as a marker, just as with my debut N.E.X.T., just as I will do with my next piece and the next one after that. Each book embodies a specific time in my life and an important milestone in my writing career. The Cozdle was good coming from the hands of a teenager. So, that is what you all get to read, the imaginings of my sixteen-year-old mind, with some brief edits by my twenty-year-old self.

I hope you enjoy the ride ;)

# THE COZDLE LEGEND

Opposing forces once will blend
Two hearts in fear shall seek to mend
These, what's of life here left inside
When bleeding skies have wept and cried.

The eyes of he shall see it through
The pace at which to seek the view.
The mind of she knows not the same
And leads them to the deepest pain.

Their trust may lead the greatest loss,
And leave them slain among the moss.
Do fear the lack of knowing best
But fear is not the greatest test.

For them we wait an endless day
Before our lives leave to decay
From darkness these two wanderers rise
To save us from this great demise.

# PROLOGUE

# THE ANTIQUITY

125 years ago our world split in two.

At one point, the Imperians and the Obsequians lived in peace; they were one.

But when the Split occurred, the war began almost instantaneously as if being on separate parts of the world changed value.

And in reality, it did.

The war raged for many years, a fight for resources, for power, for strength, a constant fighting all over what was left of the planet. And, truly, a historical war for the books, the first documented since before the spilt.

Some forty years ago, there were talks of a truce, some sort of compromise that would bring the war to a halting end and spread peace about the remains of our world.

But a young woman called Case strongly disagreed and usurped the lead position of Imperious, coronating herself as Luminary, and creating a new war, this time a war of compassion. And thus she implemented the Imperious kiss, a command of power and slight acknowledgement of victim in the wake of a kill.

The war still rages, the Imperians still kiss and the Obsequians still defend. As it may, two heirs have been selected by each side to succeed their rulers so that one day the strongest country may finally come out on top.

# PART I

# CHAPTER 1

I stand next to Luminary Case, a crystal crown sitting loosely in my long brown hair. My dress flows to the ground like waves and I look out into the empty cavern I reside in, simply taking in this moment among other things.

I don't look like the other girls in Imperious. They're all tall, blonde with blue or dark hazel eyes, and beautiful. As I said before, I have brown hair, so dark it is almost black. And my eyes are dark brown, so dark that at times it seems as though my pupils do not exist. Standing before this cavern of blond heads and sharp blue eyes only reminds me of how different I am. They all have perfectly white skin, which is cherished in Imperious. But mine is a light brown. As a result, I am considered rare. And that is why I stand up here, in royal gowns, that crystal crown sitting atop my curls, why I was selected as heir and they were not.

Every time I stand before them, I remind myself of this. I was meant to be here, all the years of fear and displacement lead me up to this. And it has with it given me all my strength. For it, I am stronger, and with that strength I will one day be their leader, their strongest if I can help it.

Luminary Case coughs. Time is getting to her. She is middle aged but with the work of a Luminary, she seems older, more worn out.

The Fidelity is about to begin. My hands become sweaty as the cavern fills with my people. This is the first Fidelity in which I will lead. Luminary Case will retire in exactly three years, when I am twenty, and I will resume her spot on the throne. At that time, the culmination of all my hard work will come to be and I will rule as I have been taught.

And win the war.

Something that has only happened in dreams.

But that will become a reality at my own hand.

"Quiet!" Luminary Case. She uses the Imperious call, a long drawn out scream that rings throughout the room, loud and blunt, just as we are known for being. As soon as the word is finished, the people quietly stare directly at her. She looks over at me, very slowly, and smiles gently.

All the eyes fall on me.

And what I will not admit was fear before, turns quickly into adrenaline and excitement. I have their complete attention and control.

I am in charge today.

"Suudella!" Luminary says. That is my name. It is tradition to use the call before a person speaks in ceremonies. As soon as she finishes, I step down onto the large platform, to the center. I stand, with my fingers laced before me, at the crowd of people around. The many thousands are divided by age group. I look around, showing the crowd that I am not in fear; just as Luminary taught me.

"Greetings, my fellow Imperians, and welcome to our annual Fidelity ceremony. Let us begin with the story of our people."

I look down at my feet. At the shiny flat shoes I wear. They match my crown…but now is not the time for distractions. I look up at the crowd placed before me and tell them the story exactly as I learned it.

"After the Spilt things changed. There was war and poverty. And hatred spread all throughout the planet. Our home, Imperious, had lost many battles and it was nearly destroyed. We were ready to give up." I notice a few sufficient nods in the crowd, a grunt here, an agreement there. I continue with satisfaction. "Our great leader," I gesture to Luminary Case. "was the only reason we came out alive, refusing to surrender, to bow, choosing still to fight. She saved us. As we began to lose sight of our own strength, she helped us realize what we needed and how to show compassion along the way, that after all the battles we had lost, we need our revenge." More nods, more noise. My voice begins to rise. "And we needed to show them who we really are and what we stand for, what we really mean!" The entire crowd screams. "Because we are stronger! We are faster! We are far more powerful! And we are Imperious!"

My speech ends to the roar of a screaming crowd.

Luminary smiles proudly and I feel accomplished with her approval. I nod gently as the crowd chants my nickname *Del, Del, Del…* and stand on my platform once again.

Luminary Case steps forward to where I stood before. As she does, I keep my head held high, as a Luminary ought to.

She stands tall, as many of the women of Imperious do, nearing six feet or taller. At this I note another of my distinctions from them. My small stature and skin have become my greatest assets. Case looks straight ahead and the crowd falls silent. She looks around at the crowd with a tight grin on her face. Her age is showing around her eyes. But somehow, I think she is rather proud of it.

"Thank you all for your attention." Pause. "And let us all applaud Del for that wondrous speech." The crowd cheers and I try to hold back a smile, to look sophisticated and important and powerful. But when the crowd stands to applaud, I cannot hold back. A small smile forms on my face and I look around at the crowd proud of myself and my strength.

I am better than them.

And they know it.

That is something to be proud of, as Luminary always says.

"Alright, alright, settle down now." Case says. The people settle into their seats and watch attentively as Case speaks. "I," she begins, "have been your Luminary for many years now. I am the first, as many of you know. And I created the name so as to have a strong separation from the Obsequious Leader," The people watch attentively as do I. She continues. "I chose the title "luminary" because it means something that gives off light. And I think of myself as light to this land. Or more like fire. Not literally of course, but I brought you all out of a dark state. I made you believe. I gave you hope.

"But soon it will be time to pass the torch to my successor, Suudella. Or as many of you know her, Del." She gestures for me to stand beside her. My heart pounds. This was not planned. She did not warn me of this. I don't know what is going on. If she has me speak I will not know what to say.

Stop it, I think to myself. I will know what to say; especially as future Luminary of this land. I will have to know what to say. I step down beside her, showing her and everyone else that I am not afraid.

I am never afraid.

"Suudella," She says directly to me, her arm across my shoulders. "Three years from now, you will wear my crown. You will sit on my throne. You will rule this land. And these people," I can feel her breath on my face as she speaks. But I continue looking ahead. "Will call you their Luminary. So, I must ask you," and she pauses again. I take a deep breath. "What strength do you have?"

There is a short silence. A slight pause as if time has frozen. Everyone awaits my answer. This is the question of Imperious. What strength do you have? I have the strength of the birds, of the hawk, of the eagle. I have the strength of the bugs that surround the ground. I have the strength of the people that listen to the words I speak and the sun that gleams orange in our dark sky. But I say none of this because there is something stronger than all of this. I stand taller, smile, and say simply and directly to Luminary Case, "I have your strength."

And the crowd goes wild.

It's past dusk. The sun is setting gently over the horizon, a giant ball of fire sliding into the dark sea. I watch it silently from my balcony. Quietly remembering the surge of power I got just from standing before my people, wishing that feeling to return.

Just then a rock hits the side of my balcony near where I sit. A rock. Someone threw a rock on top of my balcony. Instinctively, I grab one of my hand knives and tuck it under my sleeve.

Everybody chooses a weapon at Year Eight graduation when we transfer from bare-handed combat to weapon training. I knew at first sight just nine years ago that the the Veitsen would be mine. Just looking at them, at a mere eight years old, I knew that I could fully channel all of my power into them and fulfill every aspect of my destiny. My Veitsen and I are one.

I stand, cautiously looking around at my surroundings, wondering what sort of idiot would dare attempt to sneak up on me. With fire already flowing through my veins, coursing through every limb, I call out.

"Who is there?" There is no response. Not for several seconds. And then there is a rustling from a nearby bush. I refrain from jumping backward and press forward to the rail of my balcony. I look over the edge and see the bush rustle once more. "Show yourself!" I practically scream out in fear. I mentally abuse myself for being so afraid. The Luminary cannot fear. And then Lenten emerges from the bushes. My boyfriend. And instantly rage builds within me. "Lenten?!"

He nods arrogantly, like all the men—and women—of my country. "What in the world do you think you are doing?" I whisper loudly. "Visiting you," he replies casually and then leaps into the air, grabbing the lower railing of my balcony and hauling his broad body inside.

"You shouldn't be here," I say softly.

"You shouldn't be scared," He says teasingly. I stay quiet for a moment, contemplating denial.

"My mother might find you," I say instead, looking over both shoulders to ensure we aren't being watched. "or worse, my father."

"I can take your father," He says confidently. "It's your mother I'm worried about." I playfully hit his rock solid chest and laugh. My mother is no taller than five feet with a slender build, but she is one of the toughest women in our country. Lenten shifts gently and turns to face me, grabbing my wrist. The somewhat seductive smile he wears fades into a frown, a crease forming between his light colored eyebrows. "What is this?"

Lenten pulls my knife from underneath my sleeve. My eyes widen at the weapon between his lean fingers. He twirls it around carelessly. "Oh!" I begin.

"You were going to throw," he cuts in. "your Veitsen at me?!" he seems startled and amused simultaneously.

"What?" I ask defensively. "How was I supposed to know it was you and not an Obsequian." I pause, becoming entranced in his eyes for just a moment and then regain my ground. I think he may have noticed. "Or better yet? What if you were a Liable?"

"But I'm clearly not," he says accusingly.

Liables are the neutral side to the war. They don't live

in Imperious or Obsequious, they live in the woods on either side of the gaping river that divides the two kingdoms. They are savage beings and bring nothing but trouble.

"But how was I supposed to know?" I continue. He raises one of his perfectly groomed bronze eyebrows. "I grabbed the Veisten before you came out of the bush." He didn't move. I roll my eyes and turn away, hopelessly trying not to laugh as he sighs.

I hear him set my knife down and feel him come up behind me. I can feel the heat of his body against my back even before he makes contact. He wraps his lean, muscular arms around me and rocks me gently side to side, pressing his cool cheek to mine.

"You did great at the Fidelity today, Babe." I smile broadly as he presses his lips to my cheek and then gently onto my neck. "I couldn't take my eyes off of you…" He breathes into it and I shiver. I turn around and wrap my arms around his waist, looking up at him. I feel so small next to him, in his arms. It's nice.

In all honesty, I haven't known Lenten that long. I never really noticed him until a few months ago when he approached me in training. But then again, I'd never really noticed anybody. I don't know how exactly I'd missed him, but I had. I'm just glad now that he and I are together and I have someone to talk to that understands me in whatever small way he can. But one can only understand the life of the future Luminary so much.

We rock gently from side to side, just enjoying each other's presence. He leans down with his eyes shut and I watch him for a second before tilting my head up and giving him my cheek. He smiles into it and I smile too, and then he pulls back and goes for my lips again. I dodge and he hits my nose. He bends down, lifting me off of the ground and once again tries to kiss me on the mouth. I tilt my head up and his lips land on my chin. His lips are soft and cool, like the rest of him. Yet he keeps me warm in the now nighttime.

The moon is overhead and the stars spread about. He puts me down and I look up at him, and he says the words I dread. "Why won't you let me kiss you?"

"Because," I begin but he lets go suddenly and I become startled.

"No, Del, no more excuses. It's been three months!" Then gentler, softer, with more love, with more…longing. "Let me kiss you."

"Lenten," I say. "You know I've never kissed a living person before. I'm just not sure I'm ready. And besides, kissing is for our victims. It our only vulnerability."

He smirks slightly and looks me up and down as he takes a few small steps back. "I'll be your victim." And then he winks and my heart races at the slight implication of…

He pulls me in to him and his lips almost brush against mine.

"Trust me," He says. "No one has to know…" And right when his cool lips are about to press into mine, there is a hard knock on my bedroom door.

"Suudella!" My mother calls. "Dinner is ready." And when I don't answer, "Suudella! Come down. Now." And with that, she retreats from my bedroom entrance.

I look at Lenten and smile. "Save it for a more…romantic occasion," I say softly. He smiles sadly and nods, releasing me from his tight grasp. He walks over to the edge of my balcony and begins to climb down.

"Del," he calls. I look over the edge. "Meet me on the dock at midnight." I nod and smile widely as he climbs down and walks away.

It's about time I kissed the living.


When I reach the bottom of the stairs I see Luminary Case in my doorway on her way out. She says something quietly to my mother. "I don't care what you do with it. You just leave Suudella out of this!" my mother says, her voice raising. Case looks from me to my mother and then to my father and says nothing. She just raises her eyebrows and nods as she closes the door behind her. Gone.

Not a word has been said but I can still feel the tension in the room, like an eerie fog in night air. I ignore what my mother said, confused by what it even means, but my mother and father avoid making eye contact with me and frustration begins to build up in my chest.

What just happened? Why was there a meeting with Case that I didn't attend? Why are my parents acting so distantly?

"Mom," I say cautiously. "Dad, what the heck just happened here?" It comes out forcefully and exactly how I intended.

"Del," my father begins. But my mother doesn't give him the time of day. He hasn't even gotten to his second word before she's cut him off.

"Sit down, George." My father obeys my mother's command without hesitation. He doesn't even have second thoughts, he just sits by his plate and waits like a puppy. Disgraceful. At times I feel he is more of an Obsequian than anything. "Suudella Iza Calhoun what on earth gave you the audacity to speak to me…us like that?"

I feel a sudden wave of defiance. "Oh please, Mom. Don't even pretend that Dad has a say in this. We all know that you wear the pants in this family." I can't bear to wait for a response. I just turn on my heels and join my sullen father at the table.

My mother does not move. She stands where she was before, staring at the spot where I originally stood. I feel slight satisfaction at her insecurity. She turns and joins us as well in a matter of seconds, letting go of my rude comment to my surprise. All of my satisfaction fades to nothing.

I turn up my nose and pick at my food. Some nerve. I am heir to the throne and she knows it. She will bow down to me in a matter of years without hesitation, whether she likes it or not.

"Why was Luminary Case here?" I ask almost innocently. I know my power, but I don't have to use it all the time. And I know in order to get actual answers I will need to play it nice.

"Doesn't matter," My mother replies passively.

"Well I think it does, seeing that it pertains to me."

"Who told you this is about you!" My mother snaps. "This world is not about you, Del. You are not the only person living in it. And you certainly are not the only person fighting for it."

"You said my name—!"

"When I said it did not matter I meant it! Now eat your dinner and get to bed. You have a long day tomorrow." I huffed, annoyed by her refusal. But when we both thought the conversation was over, my father spoke in the smooth silence.

"Luminary Case thinks it'd be best if you moved in with her soon." My eyes widen with excitement at the thought of being away from this cage I live in, guarded by these two rats called parents.

"George!"

"What, Annabel? What now?" He almost sounds like a child. How pathetic.

"I thought we agreed—"

"We didn't agree on anything." My father says matter-of-factly as he cuts my mother off. She smiles tightly, pure frustration clear on her aging face.

"Well I am going to," I conclude.

"No." My mother said abruptly. "I didn't want you training with her in the first place. And yet here we are."

"What?" I ask.

"You heard me, Del. I never wanted you in this line of work. Ever."

"But why?" I ask. "I have the perfect life, I have power."

"And that is the problem, Del!" She screams and stands from the table swiftly. "Don't you see it, Del? And you George, you talked me into letting her! This was your idea!"

My father does not respond. He just keeps his head down and stares at his food, not eating.

"And now look at her! Look at what she's created! What

you've created!" I do not know how to respond. "She's a monster she's—,"

"What? I am no monster!"

"You are!" my mother is a step away from hysteria. Her eyes are blazing and her chest is heaving. I can practically see her heart beating through her tiny chest. This obviously is not a new realization. "Just look at yourself, Del. You are just like her!"

"Who?!"

"Like that lunatic Case! You are just like her! I cannot look at you without seeing her!"

"Which was the purpose of all of this!"

"No! No!" She pauses slightly and then continues. "I am supposed to see myself when I look at you, not that power hungry dragon." She's crying now. Her voice breaks. "You are my daughter. Mine."

"No," I say softly, passively.

"What?" her voice is a whisper.

"I am not your daughter,"

"What are you—"

"I," I say slowly, "am not your daughter. Well biologically, of course, but mentally? Emotionally? Why, I'm not related to you at all, or Dad for that matter. He's too submissive. Too…obsequious."

"You—" the anger begins to return to her apple red face, streaked with tears.

"I am Luminary Case's daughter whether you both like it or not. I am one of the most powerful alive and you will bow to me if—"

"Stop. Right now." My father. I've never heard him speak like this before, with force and authority. "You do not speak to us like that! We birthed and raised you! You will respect us!" my father yells. It's a tone I've never heard from him, never imagined possible. But I do not falter.

"You may have birthed me," I say to them in a soft, low voice. "but Luminary Case raised me."

And the best part?

I feel no remorse.

I sit in my room for hours unmoving. Motionless on my bed, I think about what I said to my parents—more so to my mother. I try to decipher my feelings, whether or not I hurt her intentionally.

I am pretty sure I did it on purpose.

I do not feel bad though. Not even an ounce of guilt rests on my chest. But shouldn't I? Should I not feel like a disrespectful waste of mass?

No, of course not. I cannot feel guilt for such a thing. Guilt is a sign of weakness. And I am most certainly not weak.

I am not exactly sure how much time has passed. I have been sitting motionless for what seems like forever, unsure of what feelings are and are not normal to who I am supposed to be.

When I hear the door to my parents' room close gently, I walk outside onto my balcony and look up at the sky. The moon is maybe about ten minutes away from the center of the sky, which indicates midnight.

After several silent minutes of waiting, the light to my parents' room finally goes out and I unhook the latch to the stairs of my balcony. I lower the steps down as slowly as possible in order to avoid clangor.

I descend the steps slowly, cautiously observing my surroundings. There is no telling who could come out of the woods behind my house, no way to know who is waiting. You'd be surprised as to who would want the heir dead…

As soon as I am within the forest trees, the noisome smell of animal feces wafts me in a cool wind. It's a scent I am rather used to yet my face contorts still. It is in no way pleasant. And yet despite the smell that surrounds me, the night is still beautiful. The moon is just past crescent; the full moon should be coming soon. That is my favorite time of the month. I somehow feel more powerful with a full moon; there is no real reason why. I just do.

I walk throughout the woods and towards the other side in complete silence and without fear. I carry my Veitsen with me at all times—I have them now—so I am prepared for a fight against any person who may approach. And yet as prepared as I am, at every sound I hear, a gust of wind, twigs breaking, bushes scratching, branches touching, I flinch. I step back. I show fear.

But fear is not to exist within me.

And yet I cannot control it.

No matter how hard I actually try, I am still afraid. I am alone, in the dark, in the woods, away from home. My parents don't know I'm gone and no one actually knows exactly where I am. If I were trying to assassinate me, now would be the perfect time to strike.

There is no one around.

Or there is everyone around.

There could be an endless amount of Obsequians watching me, standing by, waiting for that perfect moment, that perfect shot. And here I am, just asking for a lone fight, asking to be killed! What if someone really is out here? What if they have just been waiting all this time for me to think irrationally? What if...

Paranoia.

Paranoia will get me killed. It is something I've been taught to think against, to fight internally. Why now was I so...afraid?

"Just stay calm," a soft, deep voice says from behind me. It is a comforting voice, but it is not a voice I recognize. And with absolutely no hesitation, I take off in a sprint to the end of the woods.

I do not look back at the face of my stalker. That must explain my paranoia. I could feel their presence even without noise. I suppress the relief I feel knowing that my training has paid off. I am not a disgrace.

But just for safe measure, I jog the rest of the way to the dock.


The moon is just over head by the time I reach the dock.

When it comes into view, I breathe a weighted sigh of relief. And I refrain from glancing over my shoulder for fear that I am still being followed. My heart still pounds in my rib cage and my breath is heavy from running for so long.

When I finally stop moving, I scan the area in search of Lenten. The fear and paranoia within me is joined by the utter excitement of spending a night alone with him, even if it is on a dock. My heart begins to pound faster at the thought of having my first kiss. I've kissed boys before, but not like this. They weren't...alive.

When Case came to power, she implemented them as a symbol. The kiss we share with each of our victims is our way of showing the compassion it appears we lack. Because often times, we do kill in cold blood. So by kissing them, just as their heart stops, just as the haze covers their eyes, we prove that there is love in our hearts. And the victim's last moments aren't filled with hatred.

Their lives end with a kiss.

I was 11 when I kissed my first victim, after my first actual battle. I'll never forget it, the soft feel of the cooling lips of the person you've just stolen the life out of, giving them that last ounce of hope... It never gets old.

"Who are you waiting for?"

If I didn't recognize this voice, I would scream. I would spin around and thrust my Veitsen into the heart of the speaker, twist it twice and pull it out. I would wait for them to fall over. And as I would watch the glossy haze covers their eyes, and I would kiss them That's just how it works.

But this voice, I recognize. The mocking tone, the underlying sound of jealousy hidden beneath it...It can only belong to one person.

I turn around and look into the hazel eyes of Tessa, the only "friend" I actually have. Except, she's more like a person

I tolerate that tolerates me because we both are in need of someone to talk to. But Tessa, she's always been jealous of me, ever since she we were kids. She's hated every aspect of my body every waking moment of the time I've spent knowing her. And yet, we still tolerate one another's company out of desperation.

"I could ask you the same question," I reply, crossing my arms over my chest. Tessa looks like all the other girls, tall, blonde, light eyes. The opposite of me. Which is why I used to resent her. For many years I hated my appearance, the way it makes me stand out so much. Only since the nearing of my coronation have I come to embrace the power it gives me over them. Tessa is just one of many other tall, blonde girls who think it should be them on the podium with Luminary Case. But it's not. It's me.

"Yeah sure, but I asked you first."

I roll my eyes at this statement. So immature, so...juvenile. Why on earth do I put up with her childish ways? "I'm meeting Lenten here."

"Really now? Because I was just—"

"Hey, Babe!" Lenten comes up behind me and wraps his muscular arms around my waist. I turn around in them to face him and wrap my own arms around his neck.

"Hi," I say sweetly as he presses his lips to my cheek. When he pulls away, I look into his eyes as we hold our embrace. But he isn't looking at me. As I look at him he shoots a look towards Tessa, a look that I cannot read. It confuses and frustrates me as to why his attention is focused on her and not me, so I pull him into a tight hug. His grip on me tightens as he presses his lips to my neck.

"Oh, get a room," Tessa says.

"Jealous are we?" Lenten replies mockingly. I laugh at his joke and we let go of each other, both facing Tessa.

"Why are you even here?" I ask her, a little humor still prominent in my voice.

"Lenten invited me," she says matter-of-factly. Lenten shoots her another look and she smirks evilly. I let go of Lenten's arm quickly, highly offended by what I have just heard.

"What? Why?"

"Why not?" he walks away a bit, towards the water.

"That is not an answer, Lenten. Why is she—" and before I can finish, he swoops me up and kisses me on he cheek, just shy of my lips. A shiver runs through me.

This is what I came for.

But that needy petulance Tessa decided to come. Before I can continue my angered thoughts toward Tessa, Lenten kisses me again, just beside the corner of my mouth. He sets me down, still working his way up the side of my face. Then he pulls away and looks me in the eyes.

"Why she's here doesn't matter. What matters is you," he kisses my cheek. "and..." Kisses my neck. "Me." and he leans down to press his lips against mine. I can feel the heat from his body on mine; I can feel his breath on my lips. His lips just brush against mine, just barely...

But a splash comes from the water that tears us apart. Our heads spin to the source and we spot a person pulling themselves onto the dock. The three of us wait for the person to show their face. That will decide whether or not we fight, alert authorities, or leave him be.

When the intruder stands, he spots the three of us standing together. Tessa moved from behind Lenten and me to beside Lenten. I am not sure how I feel about this but that is not the problem at hand.

The problem at the moment is this man. He is not an Imperian. Not by any stretch. Just by his posture and the stricken expression he wears, it is evident that he is not from around here.

The intruder speaks. He is probably a little older than me. No older than twenty. Handsome. But not from here. "Oh goodness please, please spare me. The ship...it...oh please, for the life of me, please...don't kill me."

An Obsequian undoubtedly. The way he raises his arms in surrender, his pleading, his submission.

This will be fun...

As if on cue, Lenten begins mocking the young man's pleading. "Oh don't kill me! Oh ho no, no, no please! Don't kill me. Boo hoo hoo..." and he pouts like a child. Tessa and I both explode into laughter as Lenten goes and grabs the young man and yanks him to his knees. He pulls him away from the edge of the dock so he can't jump.

"Where you from, kid?"

"O-o-Obsequious, s-s-Sir."

"Ohh? 'Sir' I like that, has a nice ring to it, huh ladies?" Tessa and I both nod as we hold back our laughter. Lenten circles the Obsequian like an eagle stalks its prey. "So what brings you here, Obsequian. You got a name?" Lenten hits the Obsequian in the head and draws his sword. He lifts the sword to the Obsequian's chin. Tessa and I watch with anticipation.

Only women kill men in Imperious and vice versa. It wouldn't make logical sense to kill another woman for the same reason men don't kill men. There is an underlying respect for someone of your sex that is just stronger and more important than the hatred that consumes and motivates your country of origin.

And that means either Tessa or I get this one, Lenten is just warming him up.

The Obsequian finally responds. "W-w-w-Winton, s-s-Sir. M-my name is w-w-Winton." A villainous smirk spreads across Lenten's face as he snatches his sword away, cutting Winton's neck slightly in the process. The wound begins to bleed slowly.

"So, Winton," he continues cockily. "What brings you to Imperious, hmm? Did you have a nice swim?" I stifle a laugh.

"I'm looking…" his voice trails.

"What? Sorry I can't hear you through the thick cloud of your fear. You're going to have to speak up."

"I'm looking for my aunt." It comes out like it was some how exasperating to admit, more so than the fact that he was nearing his death sentence.

Lenten looks taken aback by this unusual confession. "I can almost guarantee your aunt isn't here.

"No, she is! I swear she—"

"Dude, shut up." Winton closes his mouth abruptly. "Look, it sucks that you took a wrong turn," Lenten stretches to draw out the moment. "But, I'll tell you what. Since you have been so weirdly honest, I will let you choose your match.

33

So, which one of these lovely ladies would you like to kill you?" He continues circling him like prey as he speaks. "We have Tessa," And Lenten slides over and begins advertising her, like some sort of game. And, in many ways, it is. For us, at least. "Tessa stands at about five-foot eight at a mere 135 pounds. She likes long walks by the dock and spontaneous victims from another country."

The Obsequian shivers, partly from the cold air hitting his wet skin, and partly from the fear of his imminent death.

"And over here we have the beautiful and vicious Del who may not be quite as menacing at first glance, but is definitely as blood thirsty." Lenten swaggers back over to Winton who is now shivering so much it could pass as a seizure. "So, Winton," Lenten lowers his voice. "Who'll it be?"

The fearful Obsequian looks from Tessa to me and then back to Tessa. "The s-s-short one., sir. The—"

"Well," Lenten cuts in. "Quite a choice you made there. Did I mention she's Luminary Case's heir?" Winton shakes his head vigorously as his eyes spill over with tears. "Oh, I must have…forgotten." And he smiles evilly as he glides away and over to me.

"Make it quick," he whispers into my ear and then slaps his hand against my rear end. It startles me and my eyes bulge in shock. He winks as he walks away, pulling Tessa with him and leaving me to my own devices. As they leave, I hear him say "His aunt? Seriously?" And then the both of them laugh. I laugh a little too.

At a moment's will I transition to kill mode and walk slowly up to Winton, the fearing Obsequian, making him cherish every living moment he has left. I kneel before him so we are closer to the same size, so I can look him eye-to-eye. He still holds his hands behind his back and looks straight ahead, gulping repeatedly, shaking uncontrollably. Afraid. Knowing.

"Look at me," I whisper.

He shudders at the sound of my voice and slowly trains his eyes on me, tilts his head down. I give him a vicious grin as I pull my knife from my sleeve. I twist it around in my fingers as I look at him and brush the flat end against his face. He looks as if he is about to explode.

"Make a wish," I say and just as the tears in his eyes fall faster, just as his shudders make noise and the hysteria begins…I jab my knife into his stomach and twist twice.

All of his shuddering stops, the tears stop falling, his breathing becomes staggered. But his eyes still look into mine. They plead to me. His eyes say all the things his voice cannot.

And in those moments, in those eyes I learn who Winton is. He's just a kid who got stuck in this war, just like the rest of us. A kid who wanted nothing to do with it from the start, who tried to run away, to make a new life, to be himself. But he got stuck here. He got stuck with me.

And I am merciless.

All from his eyes, I can see who he is and that he meant us no harm. But that doesn't matter. We are all stuck in the war. And there are just some things you have to deal with.

One last breath falls from his lungs and into my face. The cold, wet hands struggling against mine stop. He no longer blinks. His body goes limp against my knife. And that haze— that white haze that so easily indicates death—covers his eyes slowly.

You can see it.

It crawls across his pupils like a hand reaching to pull you down, tightening its grip and never letting go. There is an ounce of life left in him. You can feel it. He is not entirely gone, but too far gone for saving. So I brush my nose against his, brush my face against his, breathe my living breath on him.

A single act of compassion.

And then, slowly, gently, I press my living lips against his dying ones and hold them there. Until I know he's gone for good.

When I pull away, the haze has fully covered his eyes and he is unmoving. I extract my knife from his wound and lay him to the ground gently. And then silently, I roll him over the edge of the dock before dipping the blade into the water and wiping it off on my shirt.

I feel no remorse.

Yet.

As I stand over his floating body and watch for just a moment, I relive this night, the paranoia, the fear, a death, and a kiss. And I think, too, of what lies ahead for tomorrow. It could be hard. Maybe it won't be.

But I am still where I began this day, no different from the moment I woke up until now. No more experienced in any aspect.

Maybe there is a reason for this, but I do not know. Maybe there is a reason for all of this, something greater or more meaningful.

Or maybe there is nothing at all.

# CHAPTER 2

I didn't sleep last night.

As soon as I got home, I took a shower; a much needed shower in which I stood under the scorching water and let it run down my body as the events of the night dominated my brain.

I killed that man in cold blood.

That boy.

He was harmless and I knew it, yet the knife found its way inside of him just like it always does.

Coldblooded killings are always the worst. They have the most impact. And that's why now, as I walk up to the Facility, I cannot get the image of his lifeless eyes out of my head.

I was right. It was as hard as I'd predicted.

How unfortunate.

It will never go away.

They never do.

Especially the first time. Oh, that first time…

Nothing beats that first time, that feeling of holding another person's life in your hands and…taking it from them without a second thought…

It's what we do, it's what we're bred for.

We are made to kill.

The Facility is directly before me. It isn't a particularly attractive building. So many wars and fights and deaths have taken place here. But it is the place where every Imperian learns the art of war. So, for me, it is the most beautiful.

The guards in front of the doors bow their heads slightly as I approach. I suppress a slight smirk as I continue through the double doors and into the first floor of the building. Everyone does the same thing.

"Del! Del!" A tiny little voice calls from behind me. "Del!" I turn around to see the bright face of Demi, a tiny little girl of seven and one of my thirteen trainees.

"Hello Demi," I say nonchalantly. At the tone of my voice she stops and bows her head in respect. I give her a little smile and in seconds she attacks me with a hug. "Ready for today?" She nods vigorously, eager to discover what activities I have planned for them.

The rest of the group arrives and we make our way to the training.

"Alright kids, line up!" and they do so within seconds. I have trained them well. Because I am supposedly the most talented of fighters in my generation, I was gifted with the misfits. That lasted but a day, though, with my…punishments. "Buddy up!"

The kids quickly find partners when I note that there is an even number of pairs. There should be one left…

"Where is Ace?"

Ace. The misfit of all misfits. Doesn't listen to anybody. Not even myself. Uncontrollable. "I said," I raise my voice an octave. "Where is Ace?" I say the words slowly and the room goes quiet. Every voice stops in the oversized room aside from one.

"Give it to me or I swear I will kill—"

"Ace!" I scream. He stops talking, pushes his victim down onto the padded mat, and runs over to his place in line.

"Sorry Instructor Del, I was just—"

"That's enough Ace," I say softly.

"—but that little girl was—"

"I said enough!" And I scream the words. The room stays silent and everybody stares. "I have warned you enough, and because you refuse to listen, well, it's time for a new lesson, Ace."

"What kind of lesson?"

"Center Mat. Now."

"But Instructor—"

"I said now!"

And the room disperses, kids leave their separate groups to join their friends to watch the fight. Ace stands in the center of the mat as a murmur builds within the room, voices wondering: Who will she make him fight?

"Demi," I say softly. "Center Mat." And she does exactly that, standing beside Ace. She does not look afraid, she does not show fear, but more so…excitement. It's like looking in a mirror.

"Begin." I say and they take their stances.

An introduction or explanation is not needed. Everybody knows. If you screw up, and you're called to Center Mat you fight your opponent until your Instructor says to stop. And if he or she doesn't...

Ace throws the first punch. Seeing that they are seven, they don't have their weapons yet. This is bare-handed combat.

Ace throws a second punch at Demi and she dodges easily and trips him. In seconds she is on him, sending a barrage of punches at his face. He manages to get up, kicking her gut in the process.

But Demi does not falter. The kick does little to harm her and she round-houses him in the face and sends another quick hit to the back of his knees making him fall forward and allowing her to attack him vigorously once again. Ace is out of energy, he is strong but not nearly as agile and Demi has no trouble beating the life out of him. He cannot get up, he is finished, he...

"Del, say stop. Now." Lenten nudges my shoulder.

"Why should I? He's getting what he deserves."

"Del,"

"What?" I turn to face him, rage in my eyes. "Why should she go easy?"

"He already won't walk for days, Del."

"Should have thought of that before he disrespected me and wasted my time." I say, crossing my tan arms across my chest.

"He's seven. Del, so help me, if you don't call stop right now..."

"Stop!" I call, rolling my eyes. Then I glare at Lenten as I walk to pull Demi off of Ace. The boy's not moving. Demi gave him a good beating. Serves him right. "Call a nurse," And two kids take off to go get medical help as I pat Demi on the back and give her a reassuring smile. Her knuckles are raw, so I walk over to the nearest cooler, grab an ice pack and sit her on top of it as I bandage her up.

"Great job out there, Demi. You really understand the meaning of 'no mercy.'" She smiles a bit as I wrap the bandages around her tiny knuckles.

"Thanks, Del. For a second I was afraid I'd actually kill him."

"You were afraid? Never be afraid of such things! Killing is a part of us."

"I understand that, but he's from my country. I don't want to kill a person with my values. That's evil." I slam my hand down beside her, making a commotion.

"Death is evil, Demi. But sometimes we make sacrifices."

"Yeah but…Ace didn't need to be a sacrifice. Did he?"

I sigh deeply to calm my raging nerves. "No. That's why I called stop before you killed him. Any longer and he'd be dead."

That was a lie. If Lenten had not told me so, Ace would be dead. We stay silent for a moment before Demi asks me another question.

"What was your first kill like?"

It's almost out of the blue and for a moment I don't know how to respond. I think about how to put it into words.

"I was seven, and my victim was…also very young." I

41

suddenly realize now how emotional this is for me, but attempt to continue. "We fought like you and Ace did, but at one point, he had me on the ground, beaten and battered and torn apart." I pause slightly, to compose my emotions.

"Maybe we should finish this story another time," I say. I'm just not ready yet. Don't know that I ever will be.

She nods. "Okay." And then, "What about the kiss?" Demi asks curiously. I breathe sharply to expel any remaining weakness.

"I didn't kiss my first kill."

She stops asking questions after that. She just pats my hand gently, a reassuring gesture far beyond her years. Then she hops off of the cooler and joins her partner for warm-ups.

As she does so, I note that many of my peers are cutting me with their eyes. Only one approaches me.

Tessa.

"You know, you've got some guts making seven-year olds fight like that."

"You know, you've got some nerve coming over to talk to me like that," I reply.

"No person in their right mind would do that, Del."

"Oh yeah, sure. Except I did."

"Well, I would never do something of the sort. It's too coldblooded." She says with such an implication that I want to challenge her right then and there. The words hang in the air above us.

"Well," I say as I recompose. "I guess that's why you aren't the heir." And I brush past her and towards the center of the room.

"You won't be able to throw that in my face forever you know!" She calls after me. I just huff in amusement.

At lunch, Luminary Case buzzes me into her Facility office.

She is on the phone when I enter, so I stay as silent as possible. "What? No. No. I said no you lousy scoundrel! I could never say such words...You know what I want from this—" She looks up and notices me standing by the door. "We can finish this later," she says, and she slams the phone down onto the receiver.

"Good afternoon, Luminary Case," I say gently. I bow my head to her and she nods it away. "You summoned me?"

"Yes," she says. She looks tired. Her age shows more and more every day, probably from the stress. "Del," Case begins. I tense up for fear of what she may or may not say. "Various... sources have told me about a mat fight you saw to today?"

"Yes ma'am. One of my trainees was rude and unprepared."

"So you made them fight?" She cuts in.

"This was not the first offense, may I remind you. So yes, I had him fight the best fighter in his group."

"Really? The best fighter?

"Yes ma'am."

"The best? Or the one that is the most like you?"

I pause for a second, unsure of what she is implying. "I don't understand..."

"Because Demi is not the highest ranked in your group, Del. Andres is according to my list."

"Well yes, but…"

"What are you trying to pull?" She raises her voice which makes me shut-up. She stands and begins to walk toward me. "What are you trying to prove?"

"I-I'm not trying to prove anything ma'am, just doing what you would have done in this situation." I stuttered. A sure sign of weakness and fear. She smirks. She can see it, I know she can.

"Ah, so that's what this is about." Case continues to make her way over to me. "Are you bringing your own personal experiences and issues onto the training floor?"

Yes. "Of course not. Just doing what I feel is right."

"Are you sure?"

No. "Yes." I cannot look her in the eye. She knows I'm lying. But she has not called me on it. The only thing worse than being found out is being allowed to lie.

"Del, have I taught you nothing?"

I do not respond. Just glance at her slightly.

"Separate your personal ties from yourself and move on. One cannot kill venomously and be fully removed if one has not fully removed oneself."

"I just…"

"Out of my office."

"But—"

"Out!" So firm, so concise.

And without further protest, without further hesitation, I exit the office and make my way to the lunchroom, humiliated.

"Where were you?" Lenten asks into my ear after I sit down with my tray. I just shake my head, indicating I do not want to talk about it. He doesn't get the message.

"Oh c'mon. Del," He nudges my shoulder. "Where were you?"

"I don't want to talk about it," I say finally.

"You sure?"

"It's just…" I pause. "Do you think I was a little harsh earlier today?" Lenten rolls his gorgeous eyes at me before speaking.

"Well, seeing that I was the one who had to make you stop the fight, then yes. You were a little harsh."

"Well it was just because I—" But before I can continue, before I can get the words off of my chest and out of my mouth, Lenten directs his attention somewhere else. Talking about something with one of his many friends.

So, I sit and think. Maybe I was harsh. But Ace deserved it.

Every last second.

He'd been disrespecting me for weeks! He got what was coming to him. And I didn't even have to give it to him. But, even Case got on my back about it. And she hinted to…

I just don't understand. I finally felt like I was doing something right, what I've been trained to and then…

This.

The bell chimes and everyone cleans their trays and files out of the lunchroom and into the training room where we all were before. As we walk, I look at all the kids. All ages, from four to seventeen. Some of these kids I've known my whole life and some I've just met because they are so young. Some things have changed but some things haven't.

I look to Lenten who has not even noticed me since our last conversation. I think that is why I like him so much. He is the only person who doesn't treat me like royalty. He treats me like a peer; like a normal person. Sure it may bother me at times, but I'm real to him. And not some figure head.

In my thoughts, I notice the crowd I walk behind has stopped.

There is hushed conversation.

There is a loud bang.

There are screams.

And as I turn my head to see, I know this could mean only one thing.

We are under attack.


Breathe, breathe…breathe…

The boy who stands above me pulls out his sword and waves it above my head. I'm on the ground, beaten down, at a loss for breath. I stare up at him with longing eyes, hoping he'll see my fear and spare me. Hoping he'll fall for it.

"Please…" I whisper gently. He couldn't have possibly heard it. It's too loud; there are too many screams for help, pleas for life or pleas for death circling within the dull room. But he can see it, and I can see the passion in his heart changing. Changing from pure ruthlessness to pity.

Perfect.

That's just what I need.

A vulnerable moment to strike.

"Please…please don't…I…" I begin to plead. I let a tear fall down my face and he lowers his sword slightly, under my chin. He pushes the flat end against it.

"Rise, Imperian." He says. I stand slowly. My hands shake, my whole body jitters…

But when I stand fully, I start fidgeting for my veitsen again, waiting…

And then he sees it. As I strike his head with the butt of my knife, he falls to his knees and I can see the fear escaping his eyes as he sees the hatred in mine. It's amusing, watching this boy who was standing above me, with my life in his hands plead for his life as I did my own. Except mine wasn't serious. But his…the sincerity shows through every vein and every pore on his blood red face. He's practically holding his breath.

"Please!" he cries. "I spared your life! Now…now you s-spare mine! Please!"

I lean toward him slowly and his eyes follow me, analyzing my every move in hopes that I will give him the same chance he gave me. "I could," I say. "That would be the nice thing to do…" I grab his chin in my hand and look him in the eye. "But I'm not known for being nice." And just as his pleas continue, just as he's shaking his head in preparation to break away from my grasp, I jab my knife into his stomach and twist twice.

When he falls to the floor I kiss him just as a spear shoots over my shoulder. I somersault over my last victim, my seventh for the battle at hand, and land lightly onto my feet. I spin on my heels to locate the owner of the weapon thrown at me. I grasp the spear in my hand and then notice the boy in front of me. He does not charge, he does not ready himself to fight. No, this child knows his fate. And he welcomes it with open arms. He closes his eyes and waits for the spear to enter his chest. I launch it and when it does his eyes shoot open in surprise and pain. I walk over to him and place my lips against his gently as he dies.

I am bored with this. The scene is chaotic no doubt, but it is a scene I've seen many times before; person after person falling to the ground, wounded or dead. Teams of two and three fighting in groups. I spot Lenten as he takes on two at once and suppresses a smile. I see Tessa giving everything she has into a boy about twice her size and I remember why we tolerate each other.

Because no one else does.

And I just stand in the midst of it as the images of my eight victims play through my head. The first three were almost simultaneous. As soon as I made my way into the facility room, I launched myself into battle mode and killed the first three unrecognizable faces that threw themselves in my direction.

Everyone always goes for the small girl. Easy target, so they think. But I am far from an easy target.

A hand grabs my wrist right then and I find myself face to face with a boy with shimmering green eyes. He's caught me off guard and I cannot pull myself from his grasp or the grip of his eyes. Our noses barely touch as we breathe on one another.

I close my eyes to gather my wits, fighting the pull of his

gaze. If he wants to throw his life to me, then fine. Let him. It shouldn't take too long to end it.

I free myself with a kick. He's left a red handprint on my wrist which angers me more, urges me further along in this fight. But I put my knives away. Fights like these I do bare-handed until the bitter end. Better to relish in the feeling of his flesh beneath my fists, enjoy the battle at its core.

He continues to stare at me in such a way that almost throws me, like he's trying to tell me something without words. But I have seen that look many times before, full of anger, hatred, fear, and exhaustion. It is a look we both share to some extent.

He approaches me cautiously, step by step by step, as if I am some tainted animal. When he is close enough, I thrust my foot into his stomach and he stumbles backward, the wind knocked out of him. I don't bother speaking, taunting as I usu-ally do. No, not with this one. This one is different. I feel al-most bad harming him, causing him physical pain. But I look past the unusual feeling inside and make my way over to him and punch him across the face.

I will admit the boy is handsome. No older than me with dark hair and pale skin. He has defined cheekbones and a sharp facial shape with a strong build. And a pair of bright, emerald eyes. The sort of eyes that look into your soul and see everything, judge you without words.

Maybe that's what he was doing with that stare.

He spits out blood and stays knelt to the ground. I run my hands over his short hair, grab hold of it, and slam his face against my lifted knee. He falls back to the ground and I stand over him. His eyes shut for only a moment before they train on me again, not quite pleading, but trying to communicate something. It has not stopped since the fight began.

And then I find myself on the floor, the room spinning because I have hit my head. The boy lies next to me and his eyes are fixed on me still. His hand holds mine tightly, squeezing for life. But then he flips up onto his feet and without hesitation kicks my ribcage. I crumple into a ball, pain coursing through every bone in my body.

When the pain passes, I stand, still gripping my hurt side. I breathe in through clenched teeth as I go at him with all the strength I can muster. He caught me off guard again when he tripped me and got me onto the floor. I cannot let that happen again. Not if I want to live.

He slaps me across the face open handed, leaving an unpleasant sting and I kick him again in his kneecap, making him stumble backwards. The look in his eyes says it all as I realize he tripped over the body behind him. A body I failed to notice. A body that helps my cause. He falls down into a chair and I see it all clearly.

This is my only chance.

This boy is bigger and stronger than me and the only way I can win is if I use my Veitsen now. So I do. I grasp the knives in my sleeves and launch them both at top speed. Much to my dismay, he falls into the chair as he attempts to dodge them and his head snaps backward unpleasantly.

One knife misses.

The other barely cuts into his arm.

I roll my eyes.

But still he is unmoving. The fall into the chair must have

caused him to break his neck on impact. I saw it with my own eyes. The unnatural way his head snapped backwards. He's gone, no doubt. Internally decapitated.

And so I go to finish the job. There are fewer people within the room at the moment, some people have made their way outside to find new victims, but most are dead. It has been brutal on us, most of the bodies clothed in our signature black garments. This has been my ninth kill, this boy. My last for the day, I hope. I don't know that I'll make it through another.

I walk over to him, stepping over the boy he tripped on. One of Lenten's trainees. One of my people. My heart aches at the realization. Just another of the young ones lost to the war. Gone.

I take a deep breath and continue towards the boy in the chair. I did not get to kiss him on the edge of death like normal, but I will kiss him anyhow. If not for him, for me.

I stand over him, looking at him for a second. His right hand is facing up, and I notice the scars on his hands, probably from childhood battles. Scars everyone of the era possesses. I trace one of the scars on his hand as I fight away the slight connection I feel to him. Some sort of attachment I don't understand. As I touch him, I swear I feel a twitch. But I ignore it, blaming it on my exhaustion and the emotional and physical pain within me.

I run my fingers along the side of his face, treating him like all the other victims of the day. Some part of me feels bad for him, but again I push past the feeling and gather myself.

I press my lips against his. They are still warm and I can taste the blood in his mouth from the fight. It's a taste I'm rather used to but just as I am about to pull away, something happens. Something I don't understand and I get a feeling in the pit of my stomach that scares me like never before. Something that is unexplainably enticing.

He kisses me back.

And in that moment, everything stops. The room stops spinning, the pain in my side fades away with the knowledge of the dead boy behind me. All I can feel are his lips, which are soft and warm in the room and his hand as it grips around my wrist as it did before.

So many deaths in this room, so many battles...

But none of that matters because I remember none of it.

The only thing I can feel, the only thing I am knowledgeable of, and the only thing I truly care about is the fact that he is kissing me back.

When finally we pull away his nose is against mine and he looks into my eyes again, making my heart drop to my stomach. I step back and shake my head in confusion and fear and...

When I open my eyes, he is slumped in the chair as he was when I kissed him. And the hand that I swear grabbed my wrist; it sits in his lifeless lap just as it had before. Palm up.

I let out a slight whimper filled with so many continuous emotions I am sure my head is on the verge of exploding. I reach for the knife that's in the chair and then let out a scream that pours hatred; not for him but for me.

I should stab him now, but I don't. Why I don't know, but I'm too shaken too to stab and twist as I always do. I just stare at him and look around. The room is completely empty aside from me.

And him.

I scream out again and slap his life-drained face. And then I run out of the facility room, distraught and confused. When I reach the door, I remember that I only grabbed one of my Veitsen. I need to go back and get the other. When I turn around, I can't help but look back at the boy. I need confirmation.

If he sits there still motionless, it was all in my head and he really is dead as he should be.

And when I do glance back at him, he is exactly as I left him, slumped in the chair and lifeless. But when I take the first step towards my knife, I notice one thing. One thing that makes me afraid for my life and question everything that just happened. I get definite confirmation, but not the confirmation I want. I stare at it for a long time, letting everything register and my mind spin.

The boy's hand is sitting in his lap.

Palm down.

I can't see anything. I can't make sense of my surroundings. I can't move; I can't do anything, I can barely breathe.

I am somewhere stumbling alone in the facility back lot, mentally immobile.

The only thing running through my mind, the only thing I can truly make sense of is the fact that he, that boy in that chair, he kissed me.

He is not dead.

I felt his lips press back into mine, felt the pulse in them. He is not dead and never was. And worse than that, when he did kiss me back, I knew it. It registered in my brain. But still I did not move. I stayed there, against the warmth of his lips, feeling his grip around my wrist, the thinness of his fingers and the heat coming from them. I knew. But I did not push away.

And I did not finish the job.

That is what bothers me the most.

I scan the lot surrounding me. Fire is blazing nearby and the heat from it burns the bare skin of my arm. My clothes are ripped from battle but that is the least of the problems at hand. Bodies are all laid askew, Imperian and Obsequian. There is not a corner where a body is not slumped. But still my mind can only focus on one thing.

A whimper escapes my throat and I clutch my stomach. I can feel bile rising in my throat. These people, my people. The people I am to someday rule…so many of them have lost their lives because of this. And I stay standing here doing nothing! I stand in awe of the situation as if I have never seen it before because of one failed battle and a kiss…

But I have seen this before, many times before. Seeing it is nothing new.

This war has become a part of us; it is our lives. And there isn't a thing we can do about it but fight for what little life is left within us. We are all just little stars in the universe fighting for the light we have boiling inside, flickering, ready to give out at any given moment.

We are nothing.

And still, we are everything this world has left to offer.

I inhale a deep breath, filled with the scent of burning

fire and blood. Death. I can feel my knife in my sleeve as I always do, the right Veitsen the only in my current possession because I left the other in a frenzy. Its coarseness is still reassuring, makes me feel safer because I know with it at the very least I can still defend myself against anything and anyone.

Except the questioning thoughts and replaying of the pressure of that boy's mouth against my own.

I shake my head then, gathering myself to the best of my ability, and take off in a light jog towards my home. I have to check on my parents. The previous night was just one of my many tantrums. It does not change the fact that they are my only remaining family, that they love me.

I have to get to them and make sure the battle was contained to the facility area. If it reached town there is no telling what damage has been done, no way to know how much of the population is left.

This never happens. We have never been attacked before. All previous battles had been our ambush of them or battles previously consented to, agreed upon by both areas. But never like this. No one was prepared for Obsequians to attack at such a time. We are never unprepared, but this time…

Something explodes. I do not know what it is, I do not know where exactly it has come from but I am well aware that something has exploded near by. I am not shaken by it and keep moving. I cannot let myself fear until the moment I see my parents are both alive and well.

I look up into the sky. It is ash red from the fires and what seems like many other explosions. Obsequious came well prepared. This plot has been under works for who knows how long, but they had a plan. And that plan has been well executed, I will give them that.

I reach my street and a cry of pure anguish flies from within my heart. It has been burned to bits. Houses are on fire, burning away board by board. People run out and scream for help, there are cries of pain and pleas for help, but all I can do is stand and pray to God that he has protected my family.

And then I see a woman. She stands stricken near the other end of the block. Smaller being, a little stocky. She spots me and her face softens slightly as she makes her way quickly towards me. "Mom?" I say softly. And then I can fully see her face. It is her, it is definitely her, my mother, she is alive and well! She is okay! "Mom!" I cry out as I run to her as tears fall from my eyes like pouring rain. Never have I felt such relief.

She is ten feet away from me when she stops cold. "Mom?"

"Del," she whispers. And then she falls forward as her eyes fall backwards into her skull.

"Mom!" I cry. I catch her and look up to see her killer. I catch only a slight glimpse of blond hair, a pony tail, as it runs down the side of a house. I want more than anything to go after them but...

I extract the knife from my mother's back. She is still breathing, but barely. "Mom, Mom. You're going to be okay. I promise. Everything is going to be okay." I cannot keep my voice from shaking as I speak.

"Del," is all she says. But her eyes say so much more, so many lost I love yous and memories play in them and my tears fall onto her lifeless face.

Another cry builds within my chest as I scream, holding her body against my bosom. She has become another dead body, killed by the war. Killed by this wretched history we call our own, my own mother. Lost.

I lay her body down. Knowing that she will not be given a proper funeral breaks my heart into little pieces ripe with hatred. I hold her hand in mine and pray before letting her go completely and accepting the death lain before me.

I kiss her forehead gently and then stand. My house is less than a block away and I am afraid of what I may find. My father is in there. I don't know where or in what condition and part of me is too afraid to find out. I have already lost one, I cannot bear to lose another.

But in seconds, I find myself at my front door. It is ajar.

Someone had been inside.

I ease my way in slowly, to avoid notice. I do not want to draw attention to myself if someone is still inside. As I do so I hear a body stumble and fall, pushing a table in the process. When I am fully entered, I see my father holding himself against the wooden coffee table. I run to him, kneeling beside him. But he does not look at me, in my eyes. No. He looks out the side window with blazing eyes. And when I look into that direction I catch a glimpse of that same ponytail of blond hair.

I stand to run after that person when my father tugs at my arm gently. "Del, don't. It is not someone you want to see."

"What do you mean?" I ask as my voice begins to shake again.

"Just don't." he whispers inaudibly. He holds his hand to his side and when I look to it, it is drenched in blood. "Del,"

He grunts. "Your mother…"

I just shake my head. He nods and his acceptance breaks my heart further, how he could just take it so easily.

"Del, remember that we love you." He closes his eyes in pain and sucks in a sharp breath. "We always will." I lay him on the floor and place a pillow beneath his head. I just sit beside him and watch as his breathing slows.

His last words will never leave me.

"You can save us."

And with one last breath, he falls into the eternal sleep.

I rise slowly and make a decision then. I make my way outside and run to my mother's body and drag it back to my home as gently as I can, lay her next to my father.

I could not bare it if they were separate. I hold my father's hand and say another prayer before kissing his forehead and then leaving the house.

But I can stay here no longer for the pain it inflicts is much too deep, too deep for even me to handle.

I may never come back.

I do not plan to.

I sit against a tree. The ground is wet with dew and my eyes are wet with the tears I refuse to let fall. All aspects of strength and wisdom, everything I have learned by becoming the heir stays within me.

I will not cry.

Ever.

That is not something I, Del Iza Calhoun, am capable of. I

have to stay strong; I have to hold it in. The emotion, pain, and turmoil, they will all aid me in battle. That is all that matters at the moment. Winning.

And so I sit against a tree, freezing in the night air because I could not bring myself to enter my room and grab a sweater, no, not after witnessing my parents' deaths. I cannot go into that house, so I will sit here and freeze to death if I have to.

It will ease the pain.

I rest my head against the trunk of the tree and shut my eyes towards the sky. The air is cold and crisp, so sharp it cuts through the woods like a blade. I take a long deep breath in attempt to calm my raging thoughts. I am tied together by a thread. One pull and I may not be able to control what I do, my emotions…they'd get the better of me.

A few drops of water land on my face and I open my eyes to find that it is beginning to rain. The sky is crying. At least that's what it seems to me at the moment. And it has every reason to cry, in my opinion. The city has become chaotic and the sky is simply releasing its emotions in hopes that that will fix everything.

Just a little rain, a metaphoric tear, praying for catharsis. I stay seated on the ground, feeling the wetness of the rain as it covers me, and look down at my hands. There is a story in these hands: A story of hatred. A story of love. A story of loss…

I stare down at the blood and bruises from today, now just a horrid memory from the past. And then, I watch as the rain proceeds to wash it all away piece by piece. The dried blood becomes runny and then falls down the sides of my hands, eager for escape.

I'd like to escape.

But there is nowhere left for me to go.

I don't even know who's left or who's still alive. As far as I know, only me.

Me and that…

That boy is alive. And he is out there somewhere, he's probably waiting to run into me and finish me off. I welcome it. I feel as though I have lost all purpose. What do I have left to fight for?

But I dismiss the idea of him still living. It was just a trick of the mind I'm sure. Except I'm not sure. I have no idea what to believe or what's left to believe.

I'm just done.

And so I sit back. I close my eyes. And I wait for someone or something to find me.

"Come on," A soft voice says near by. My heart races at the sound and I begin to gather myself again. "We should be safe here." They aren't talking to me but they might as well be. Because I know that voice. I know that voice so well and I want nothing more than to run up to him and have him take me in his arms. I want to feel his warmth against me as he whispers that everything is going to be alright.

But that is not what happens.

"I can't believe it took this long." Another voice. A different voice. Female. And it too, I recognize, the way every sentence is a sneer, the rough and shrill annoyance of it.

"What do you mean?" He asks.

"Oh please," She cuts in. "I've had to watch you act like you love that skank for months, waiting for the right time for all this."

"We just…had to find the right time—"

"Yeah whatever. Let's just keep it moving before someone sees us," I edge closer until I can see their faces, illuminated by a single lantern, his wet curls and her soggy ponytail. I suddenly need physical confirmation of what's happening. I don't want to believe this. They don't even notice I'm watching.

"No one should be able to find us here. There's too much—"

My cover is blown when a disoriented whimper that I have been subconsciously holding in escapes me. Their heads spin around and that's when he sees me. That's when false compassion overrides his face.

"Lenten," I breathe. The rain now pours heavily, as do the feelings inside of me. Everything is clinging to my body like glue and I shiver painfully.

"Del," He says, taking a step toward me.

"No!" I scream. "Don't you come near me!"

Tessa does not attempt to hide her satisfaction. She exudes utter happiness at my internal pain. "What is this?" I ask. I can't even look him in the eyes.

"Del, I—"

"You know what?" I shake my head.

"Del…" He says quietly. But I can't look at either of them, can't even imagine…

So, I run.

Deep into the woods I sprint and stumble in the dark and pouring rain alone. I keep screaming at the top of my lungs, giving away my location to any predators because that is the only way I will allow myself catharsis. Not with tears, only noise.

And then I trip. Over a branch or a rock or a log or something that is capable of tripping. But once I hit the ground, I have no desire to get up, no motivation to help me to my feet. There is nothing at all. I am empty. And so I lay here, breathing in the soaking earth, letting the rain and cold cover me, imagining the angry tears streaming down my face aren't there. I hope I drown in a puddle tonight.

I hope it ends.

I feel my eyes getting heavy when I hear a scream far off. It sounds like it's coming from where Tessa and Lenten were. Serves them right, I think. What goes around, comes around.

And that statement could not be more true.

Because just as a laugh arises from within my aching body, just as my mood lightens just a little, a knee digs into my back, hands grip my neck, and a voice speaks.

"This is going to hurt a little."

There is a sharp pain in my calf, a surge of liquid throughout my veins, and then, nothing.

Nothing at all.

# CHAPTER 3

I wake up in a cage. The sun is just over the horizon and the sky looks as if it's on fire. The rain has stopped but the clouds still float overhead, ominously burning in the morning sky.

I feel like a caged animal, in some sort of animal viewing area, like a zoo. Zoos are no longer in existence, mainly because many animals are no longer in existence thanks to the war. Animals have been used as target practice for decades.

There is hay beneath me. I am most certainly being kept as an animal. My head pounds within my skull and I pull myself up against the nearest bars to sit up. I can barely hold my head up on my shoulders as I attempt to gather the events of the previous night. I can't remember anything past falling in the mud, lying there and breathing it in. Everything else is black. And then the next memory is here, like some part of my night is missing, or has been stolen. I can't remember where I am or why, how I got here or what happened to me while I was out.

I quickly check my sleeve for my knife only to find that it has been confiscated. I groan and roll my eyes before looking around as quickly as my head will allow and note that there are several other cages with people in them. We are outdoors, in some sort of...cellar or holding cell. And then I understand.

I have been imprisoned.

But by whom?

And at that moment, the door of my cage opens and two men dressed in brown rags and animal hides caked with dirt and blood stumble in. I can barely follow them with my eyes, let alone make an escape. I can't even will myself to try.

"Rise, girl," one of the men says. I stay seated. I can still manage defiance. "I said rise, girl," he repeats. When I don't, the other man yanks me up and my head spins. I can't focus on anything at all. I just see colors and spinning, spinning, spinning...

"Just as the Colonel predicted, still hung over," The first man says. "Come on, sweetheart," He leans in closer to me and says in a loud whisper, "someone would like to meet you." And then he pulls me out of the cage.

As we walk, I am able to figure out where I am, where I have been taken. I am in Liable country. The people, they are dirty, filthy even, tired, hungry, lost. There are children, mothers, fathers, entire families...traitors. Those who refuse to fight in the war live like this, exiled from their own countries.

Real target practice, I think cruelly. Animals in the way of the fight.

I am dragged into some makeshift building. It was once a hospital, I can tell by the sturdy structure, the firm build, and glossy floors, though now they are caked with grime and dirt. And it is not sturdy anymore, crumbling day by day with its age undoubtedly.

They toss me into a chair in a dark room with only a light overhead. They don't even bother to tie me down; I'm still too weak from whatever they injected into me to make an escape. Two people walk in, at that moment, and stand before me. I am trying to lift my head slowly to make eye contact, when one of them grabs me by the head, yanks it back, and then proceeds to force a liquid down my throat. I am too overwhelmed to protest, speak, or fight back. I am useless. The substance burns like liquid fire as it trails down my throat.

The woman who sent this acid down my esophagus is definitely not from around here. Not a Liable, judging by the long, white coat she wears. And the man as well, standing straight in a forest green jacket, pins located on his right-side pocket. A hat of the same color sits atop his graying head of hair and a blank expression is spread across his tightly stretched face. Something about him seems familiar…

This is the Colonel I presume, and I manage to speak, barely, but some form of English does indeed leave my mouth. "What…did…you…do to me?" the last word is forced out and all of them are slurred. I can't keep control of my tongue; it's being lazy, dragging against my teeth and the roof of my mouth.

"Simple," The man replies with a raspy voice. "You're drunk, kid." At the confusion on my face, he continues to explain. "You were injected with alcohol. You woke up this morning with what people in the past might call a hangover. What you drank right now? Vodka. The ultimate inhibitor of this generation."

The room is spinning again. Around and around and around in circles…

"Listen kid," The Colonel says. "I only need one thing from you." He pauses and lifts my drooping head to meet his eyes. "What has she told you?"

But before I have a chance to reply, before I have a chance to register the stomach wrenching smell of his breath and comprehend his question, I feel the ground against my face and hear a grunt of frustration.

I barely catch the words, "I'll handle it," before everything is lost.

I wake up in the same cage, this time, during the night. I have no memory of what took place in the day. From what I can remember, there is a five-minute difference between morning and night.

I am somewhat capable of moving my head this time; the extra sleep helped it all to wear off. So, I take this opportunity to look around and take in my surroundings. It's too dark to fully make sense of where I am, but I am guessing I am in the same spot as before, judging by the sky and the location of the moon.

Suddenly, a hand clamps around my wrist from the other side of the prison gate I lean up against. I gasp in fear and feel my heart racing in my chest at contact. All of the fearlessness I have worked to gain over the years has worn to nothing in the last twenty-four hours. So, I allow myself to hyperventilate within my fear.

"Hey, easy, easy," a soft voice says as someone pries the fingers from around my wrist. "There we go. All yours again." I can hear a slight smile in their voice, thus causing me to anticipate the chuckle that follows afterward. I rub my wrist between my fingers and slowly turn to face the speaker.

I look at his face through the rusty bars of our adjoined cages. He is young, not much older than me with oily, dirt-filled hair that he pushes back with his hand. His face is pre-dominantly clean, but his hands show how long ago his last washing actually was. "I'm Hector," he says and sticks his hand and all its filth through the bars that separate us.

I shake my head, indicating that I am not, under any cir-cumstances, shaking that hand. The slight smile that he wears fades away slowly. "You new?" he asks. I nod my head, still rubbing my bruised wrist. Whoever it was that grabbed it has a really firm grip. I watch his eyes as they follow my arm down to where my wrist is and he watches as I soothe my pain for a moment.

"Sorry about that," he says. "Phillip can get a little… touchy at times. Can't you, Phil?" He pats an old and wrinkly man on the shoulder who then relocates his frail body into a corner. "Not much of a people person," and he chuckles again, a noise that seems to come out of him regularly. I smile slightly and then turn my attention back to my wrist. I don't want to talk at the moment, let alone to a complete stranger.

And, as if on cue, Hector begins again. "You don't talk

much, huh?" I shake my head a little too quickly for my condition and wince in pain.

"Not much to say," I whisper. The words come out of me involuntarily and I become frustrated with myself for condoning conversation.

"Yeah," he replies airily. He then leans back against the wall behind him, crossing his legs in front of him at the ankle and clasping his fingers behind his head. "You got that right."

But I sit there and look at him for a minute, studying him. He doesn't look like a Liable, but he doesn't look like an Imperian or an Obsequian either. He's different, doesn't quite fit the standards of any.

He is handsome, now that I look at him; his hair is a chestnut brown and he has hazel eyes on golden brown skin. Not too muscular, but not scrawny, just normal. Yes, very handsome indeed. But still…different.

He catches my eyes before I realize he is watching me watch him. The smile on his face makes me uncomfortable and I look away for a moment. But it's not long before I have to ask. "Where are you from?" He chuckles once again before answering.

"Around," he says playfully. But from the sly expression he wears, I can tell that's about all he's willing to give. "I… travel," he says after a minute and his hazel eyes glimmer in the moonlight. I nod slightly and then look at my wrist for the millionth time, this seems to be my safe spot now; the only place I can look without being questioned.

When I glance back at Hector, he is looking at me, and I

get the feeling he has not looked away. I become uncomfortable at the thought and shift against the fence. I quickly ask another question to shake the mood; it's less awkward when he's talking.

"So, how long have you been here?"

"Six glorious months," he answers without hesitation. He looks straight ahead for a second and then back toward me. He quickly makes note of the stricken expression on my face. "Don't worry," he says softly, leaning in a little. "They'll let you go sooner if you give them what they want." He leans back again and looks toward the sky, visibly thinking. While he does, I notice the various bruises along his neck and jaw line, the knife cut on the side of his arm. The alternative is clear: refuse to admit, refuse to give them what they are asking for, and you may just barely make it out alive. This boy has been through hell.

"Well, what are they looking for? What do they want?" I ask.

"Hey, what did you say your name was?" He leans towards me again, and I take a breath.

"Del," I say confidently. It's the only thing I'm confident about these days. The only thing I am certain of.

"Del?" He asks. He seems surprised. "As in Suudella Calhoun, heir to the throne of Imperious?"

"Yeah," I say as surprised as he. "How did you know that?"

He smiles wickedly, cocksure in a way that he hasn't shown yet. "I get around." And then he winks before leaning back against the wall one more time and chuckling so much it could pass for actual laughter. "Well Del, heir to the throne of Imperious," he says. "Welcome to the slave camp."

# CHAPTER 4

The following morning, I am awakened by a tap on my shoulder.

"Hey, hey Del. Wake up. They're coming..." It's Hector no doubt, but for a moment I wish it were Lenten. That is, until I remember...

I manage to sit up in the hay of my animal pen and look toward Hector. "Who's coming?" I ask him softly.

"The Liable soldiers. They're bringing the new prisoners." I follow his gaze to a group of people stumbling into the camp single file, chained by knotted ropes. Some people are being carried and I assume that is how I made it inside.

It's only then that I realize that I heard Tessa scream, which means that they might be here already, or coming in this next batch of prisoners. But my excitement soon fades at the thought of seeing them. My emotions are a wreck since that night. I couldn't bare the sight of either of them.

"You may just get yourself a cage mate today, Love." Hector says with a wink. "Too bad it's not me." I huff at his flirting. How can he act so nonchalant in a place like this? Why does he appear to be enjoying his imprisonment?

The new prisoners begin filing by and I watch eagerly. For who, I'm not exactly sure. Anyone I know could walk by at any moment, and that's exactly what I need right now, a friendly face. Someone I know I can trust.

And for once, I get exactly what I ask for. I can see her from here and at the sight of her, I can't contain my utter happiness. Demi, my favorite trainee, is only fifteen yards away from me. "Demi!" I call out. But before I can scream again, Hector pulls me down, covering my mouth with his dirt covered hands. My eyes water, from the pain of hitting my back against the bars, as much as from not being able to reach her.

"If they know you want her, she'll be taken to the other side of camp so keep quiet." And then he releases me, retreating to the opposite end of his cage. I crawl to the painted brick wall in the back of my cage as I fight back the tears, sitting with my back against the wall and hugging my knees to my chest, praying that God gives me this one thing, this one ounce of hope. That He loves me enough to give me this one little speck of happiness in all that I've been through.

And He does.

Because as the line stops, every cage entrance has one person in front of it, waiting to be let inside. And Demi is directly in front of mine. I try with everything I have not to look at her, not to show the compassion I have for her, to ignore the fact that one of the people I care about most will be here with me. I'll no longer be alone.

One by one, the prisoners are untied and thrown into their cages unwillingly. It seems like forever before they get to mine. Seems like they know how much I need this. But finally, Demi is untied. She stares directly at me, bruises and scratches on her face, tears in her big, brown eyes.

The cage door opens and one of the guards picks her up and tosses her inside like a sack of trash. It takes all the energy inside of me to keep from rushing to her aid. She looks at me for sympathy, asking for help. She is so young.

But I look away from her, resting my head against the bars beside me. I look to Hector who nods with approval. I will have to wait until the guards have all dispersed before I can go to her. It's the only safe way.

I become frustrated with such knowledge. I will have to sit and watch this child, as she waits in pain for me to approach her. I am so focused on the emotions within, that I almost don't see Lenten and Tessa pass me by.

But they aren't tossed into a cage…no.

They are escorted into a room and greeted by the Colonel.


It's mid-day by the time the guards leave.

When the last guard is out of sight, I stand slowly and make my way over to Demi. Walking is a challenge. It has been so long since I last stood that my limbs are stiff and it hurts to move.

Demi is in tears. She has been since she curled up in the corner furthest away from me. I sit on my knees in front of her and place my hand gently on her back. She does not turn to look at me. "Demi? Demi, it's okay now. You're okay, I'm here." She still doesn't move. "I'm sorry I couldn't help you. I just had to make sure they wouldn't separate us…" And at that she turns slowly to face me. I get a good look at her face. Oh yes, she fought very well in battle. Very, very well.

"Del…it was so bad. I was so alone and…" She begins sobbing again, harder than before, and I pull her into me.

"I know. It was bad. It was very bad. For everyone." Her miniature body shudders against mine and I lean against the wall once more and rock her gently.

Never in my life have I shown someone so much compassion. Other than Lenten, I've never shown any sort of affection towards anyone. But there are some moments when you let go of everything, even your own pride, for the well being of another person. This is one of those moments.

Finally, Demi gathers herself and pulls away from me. She sits back on her knees and stares at me. "What happened to your face?" She asks. The question catches me off guard. In all this time I hadn't thought once about my appearance until now. My face is probably filled with dirt and blood and bruises all over. And my hair…why, I must be a complete and total mess!

"Same thing that happened to yours!" I say playfully and she manages a little laugh.

"Yeah, I guess so." And then she looks down in thought. I can't tell what she's thinking about but it couldn't possibly be good.

"Do you want to talk about it?" I ask.

She shakes her head. "I fought. I won. Everyone was

scattered and running from the fire. I couldn't find my parents. Ended up lost in the woods. And then here." She pauses slightly, drawing something in the dirt beneath us with a piece of hay. "Same as everyone else."

That takes me back. I missed so much in the training room with that boy. I don't know how long I stood there with my lips pressed against his. But hardly anyone was left by the time I made my way outside.

I failed them.

I probably could have helped the situation if I hadn't been so caught up, so distracted…

So afraid.

I see Demi's hand moving in the dirt in my peripheral vision and look down at what she is drawing. It's some symbol, but doesn't appear to be anything particular. It looks kind of like a swirl that was cut in half and shifted so one half was higher than the other. I've never seen anything like it.

"What's that?" I ask.

"The symbol of the Cozdle," She says gently, there is a sort of longing in her voice that I cannot place.

"The what?"

"The symbol of the Cozdle." This, from Hector. I hadn't realized he was listening..

"What's that?" I ask. I grab Demi's hand and pull her with me as I move towards Hector.

"The legend. The legend. You've never heard the story of the Cozdle?" He seems surprised at the thought, like every person in history knew this legend. And I was somehow weird for never hearing of it.

"I hadn't either," says Demi. "until on the way here. Everyone was talking about it. Some of the captured Liables."

"I thought the Liables were running this camp?" I say.

"No," Says Hector. "Some...others are. Off the map. And some of the Liables joined them. The rest are just like you. Prisoners."

I am so confused. I don't understand why so many people know of this and I've never heard the name, not once. "Well, what is it, this legend you were talking about?" I ask them. "What does it say?" On cue, both of them immediately recite the same poem.

*"Opposing forces once will blend*
*Two hearts in fear shall seek to mend*
*These, what's of life here left inside*
*When bleeding skies have wept and cried.*

*The eyes of he shall see it through*
*The pace at which to seek the view.*
*The mind of she knows not the same*
*And leads them to the deepest pain.*

*Their trust may lead the greatest loss,*
*And leave them slain among the moss.*
*Do fear the lack of knowing best*
*But fear is not the greatest test.*

*For them we wait an endless day*
*Before our lives leave to decay*
*From darkness these two wanderers rise*
*To save us from this great demise."*

There is a long pause before anybody speaks. We all just let the words sink into our souls, our minds, and our hearts.

"What does that mean?" I ask, breaking the silence between us. Demi shakes her head as Hector speaks.

"No one actually knows. The only thing we actually know is that—"

Demi cuts him off. "Two people, a man and woman or boy and girl are supposed to save us."

"From what? Save who?" But they both shrug. "So you're saying that there is a legend spread across the world and no one actually knows exactly what's supposed to happen?"

"Relax, Del." Hector says nonchalantly. "It's a legend, not a prophecy." He stands in his cage and stretches. He is much taller than he looks, strong, sturdy. "It's just a story that's been passed down for a few generations. For hope."

"Then why have I never heard it before?"

"You're an Imperian, Del." He says teasingly. "Do you really need hope?"

I can't help but crack a smile at his wit and grab a handful of hay and launch it at him. "Hey," he says playfully. And then, "You know, it'd be really easy to take over and rule both kingdoms now." I nod. It's a little random in comparison to what we were talking about before, but I ignore it. "Maybe if we both get out we can run it together." He winks and I laugh. For a moment everything is okay.

But then the door to my cage opens, and I make eye contact with the guard who walks in, knowing instantly that he is here for me. My heart sinks in my chest, but I stand willingly. When I do so, he turns around and I follow him out of the cage.

He grabs hold of my arm and yanks me along the path leading back to the hospital. I look at Demi before my cage is out of sight and give her a reassuring smile, thankful that she didn't protest against the guard or me. She let it happen despite what she has been taught and what she wants. Hector salutes me with a smirk and I turn and face forward with a strength that I lacked before.

It isn't long before I am in the same room as the last time. But now, I am sober. I can think fully. I am myself. They don't know what's coming to them.

A lady in a white coat, different from the last woman, walks in with a clipboard. I do not attack her despite not being tied down. I just wait. It is better to wait. "Follow me," she says. I stand and walk closely behind her into another room.

But this one is different. It is larger than the first, and it is duller, even scarier than the previous in terms of appearance. The chair in the middle is completely metal and connected to the floor. It has arm straps and a basket shaped headset hanging above it. The woman forces me into the chair.

It is cold to the touch and I can't help but fight back against her as she straps me down. I wince in pain as she tightens the strap on the wrist I bruised last night. I glare at her as she continues, plotting against her, waiting for the right moment to strike. But I wait too late. And she leaves with a satisfied expression that makes me fear for my life and everything I have left.

After she is gone I look around frantically and locate a window on the opposite end of the room. A light goes on behind it and the Colonel looks at me directly. I should have known.

"Hello again," he says. "Let's play a little game." I know instantaneously that this cannot be good. "I'm going to ask you a question. If you answer it, I'll move on to the next one. If you refuse to answer, I will press this button," He presses it and electricity flows from the chair I sit in. I squirm in pain; it's like fire shooting through my veins. When it stops, I struggle for breath.

"And every time you don't answer, the voltage goes up." I wait for a higher voltage shock, as an example, but thankfully it does not come. Only the first question. "What is your name?"

"Del Isa Calhoun."

"Very good. Where are you from?"

"Imperious."

"Excellent. See how easy this is?" I glower at him through the glass as he asks the next question, a question that is undoubtedly unanswerable. "What do you know of Luminary Case's project?"

I frown in confusion. "I don't understand..." But before I can finish, electricity shoots through me, more than the last time. He's already putting the voltage up.

"Try again, kid. What do you know?"

I wait a second before answering, aware that no matter

what, I will feel more and more electricity, more pain, more fire. "I don't—" And again more voltage. I have never felt such pain in my life and I know without a doubt there is no escape for me. My death will be without honor.

When I don't answer a third time, the Colonel lowers the basket helmet onto my head. I cannot avoid it no matter how hard I try. "I don't think you'll enjoy this much. So, why don't you answer the question? I know you know the answer, Ms. Calhoun. You're her right hand. So let's save us all the trouble and just have you tell us what the heck has been going on. Otherwise...you might go brain dead today. Lobotomized." I close my eyes awaiting the pain in my brain, remembering everything I want to remember for my last moments. This wasn't fair. I have been given no time to think. Everything has happened so quickly it's like, like someone told him I know. But I don't. I don't have any clue as to what he is referring to.

"What do the kisses do?" He asks.

"The what?" But this time I'm not cut off by the electricity. This time, I'm cut off by what sounds like gun fire. And fighting. And screaming.

And then the lights go out.

I sit in the dark, motionless by force, hoping that some form of light turns on. And then I feel hands on my wrists. I stay unmoving until one hand is fully free before I remove the helmet and then punch whoever is touching me in the face. "Who are you? What are you doing?" I yell at them. But something stabs into my upper thigh and I begin to lose feeling in my body.

"I'm saving your life," they say.

And suddenly I can't move, catatonic. Whatever they injected into me has me paralyzed, but something about the person speaking throws me off, something familiar, vague, but familiar.

I recognize it.

I've heard it, only once before. But I remember.

It's the voice from the woods.

Everything's blurry...

I can't see...

...There's chaos outside...

Cages open...

...People fighting...

I look for Demi...

...Demi...

...Demi...

I see her.

Over...over there...screaming...being.

Being carried a-away.

By whom?

I can't see can't see can't see.

Everything is blurry.

I'm not walking. I'm being carried.

I can't see.

I can't see.

I can't...

# PART II

# CHAPTER 5

I am awake. I am awake but I cannot see. My eyes are closed involuntarily by a piece of cloth wrapped around my head. I attempt to take the blindfold off with my hands, and realize that they too are tied in front of me.

That is not going to stop me.

I use my abdomen to pull myself into a sitting position. I must be outside. The air is clear and I can feel sunshine on my face. I don't know how long I was out, but there is heat on my face and dirt beneath my body. I must be in some part of the forest. That is the only explanation, I presume.

I try to stand. I tuck my legs and feet as close to my rear as possible and use the muscles in my thighs to push myself up. It is much harder than I expected and I fall over on to my back in my attempt. I can't reach my hands to my face in order to take off the blindfold, and I can't get myself to stand.

I will need to use another strategy in order to free myself of this bondage.

I groan out loud, on purpose. I want my kidnapper to come out, to see what's wrong, try to fix it, help me stand so then I can fight them, kill them, and make a run for it.

When no one approaches I groan again, louder. If they don't come to help me, they will at least come to shut me up. They most likely will not want our location given away. Finally, I hear footsteps on the dirt, soft, light-footed, well suited for travel.

"Del? Are you awake?" The voice says gently. Despite their kind tone, the slight inflection of compassion, I do not trust them. And I won't; especially if they already know my name. I breathe in deeply so as to not ruin the chances of them taking the blindfold off me, and nod my head.

Suddenly, I feel knees on either side of me. I am confused for a slight second before I understand what's going on. Who-ever he is, he is straddling me so I can't escape, pressing his knees into my sides and sitting on my diaphragm.

"I am going to take the blindfold off okay? But I need you to stay put..." His voice trails in doubt and he is right to feel this way, because the first chance I get, he is done for.

The blindfold comes off only half way before I attack, using my tied hands to strike him under the chin. I did not get to see his face, but if I don't it makes it that much easier for me to kill him.

He is still on top of me after I hit him, but he makes the mistake of helping me to my feet. He yanks me up harshly and I feel my shoulder sockets pop with the motion, leaving an indescribable pain in each arm. But I cannot let that stop me. I turn around to attempt to run, but he grabs me from behind, his arms wrapped around me so tightly I can't move.

I throw my head back and head-butt him. As he lets go I then quickly follow with another punch in the face with my tied hands. He is thrown off balance and stumbles backwards. I still can't see, but I throw out my leg and get a lucky kick and he tumbles to the ground.

But he's quick and up in seconds because I can feel him standing in front of me, breathing. "I don't want to hurt you—" But I don't let him finish because I again throw a punch with both hands. It does nothing but give me time to dance around him enough to bring my arms over his head and around his neck to choke him.

I hear his satisfying lack of breathing, and let myself smile a little. I do still retain some form of control, even while half blindfolded. But then he gets a firm hold on my arms and throws me over his head. I land roughly on my back, small sticks cutting through my shirt and skin, pain shooting through every limb of my body.

He again straddles me, one hand holding both of mine to my bosom, while the other rips the rest of the blindfold off of my face. We make eye contact and I almost scream at what I see. My heart stops, my stomach churns inside of me, and I lose breath altogether.

His voice is from the woods.

His eyes are from the Obsequian battle, of the same shimmering green.

And the feeling in the pit of my stomach hasn't changed.

It's him.

The boy I kissed.

The one that kissed me back.

He survived.


It's mid-day and I have been sitting in the same position for more than four hours; legs crossed, arms tied, facial expression blank. I don't want to move, I won't let myself move, and I am not going to move. If my being uncomfortable makes him uncomfortable, then I will stay this way for an eternity.

His name is Cos. After our tussle, he sat me down near a tent and went inside. Since then, he has come out sporadically saying things like, "It's okay to talk," or, "You don't have to sit like that if you don't want to." And then, finally, he told me his name. Cos.

And now, he is sitting beside me, eating something I cannot identify, offering me a bite every now and then. I refuse despite my growling stomach. I don't trust him. So, I won't eat.

Thinking about trust suddenly brings thoughts of Demi and Hector. I wish they were here with me rather than this lunatic more than anything. At the least, I hope Demi is okay. She's young and still fragile despite her training and I just hope she is as strong as I make her out to be. Hector I'm not so worried about, and despite only knowing him for about a day, I almost miss his wit. He made the day a little bit more…interesting.

"Are you sure you don't want any of this?" Cos asks for

the umpteenth time. I turn my head away from him in refusal. As if on cue, my stomach growls in frustration. "Seems like your body is telling you otherwise." He says playfully, he looks at me for a second, but I do not meet his gaze. "Well, I'll tell you what. I am going to leave this here," He sets a travel pot with white rice in it onto my lap. "And when you're ready, you can call me out and I'll feed you."

I glare at him through the slits in my eyes and toss the rice off my lap with my knees. It lands face down in the dirt and my heart and stomach ache at the sight of it. His jaw tightens as he stares the waste of food sprawled across the dirt before us. But all he does is shake his head and walk away.

Five minutes later, he comes out with a pack on his back, a gun in his belt, and a compass in hand. "Where are we going?" I ask. I realize suddenly that I have broken my silence. But the idea of standing makes my brain fill with excitement and joy despite the situation.

"She speaks!" He says. I do not like his playful tone. He kidnapped me and thinks this is some sort of joke. The excitement in his eyes fades at my expression. He kneels beside me and looks me in the eyes. I look back into his with an attempted air of hatred before I can't help but soften my expression. His eyes…

"*We* are not going anywhere," he says softly. Then he looks down at the compass in confusion. "But *I* am going to find us some more food, seeing that you wasted half of dinner." He glances at the pot of rice still located in the dirt, now being over run by little critters from nearby. I roll my eyes as he stands. "Don't go anywhere," he says. "I'll be back in a few."

He expects me to stay here, I think. How cute.

When I think he has gone far enough, I struggle to my feet. This time I have the tent as my aid and am standing tall in no time. I look around for the best way to travel. I don't want to go in the same direction that he did in order to avoid running into him, so I go through the trees to the left.

The clearing where we were disappears in no time and before I know it, I am submerged in the trees and brush of the woods. I just keep in a straight line as long as I can, putting as much distance between myself and the camp as possible.

I look down at my tied hands and wonder how I will defend myself like this. It didn't quite work the last time. I look around for something I can possibly cut the twine off with and see nothing. I try rocks and branches and tree bark, but nothing works well enough, nothing even makes a dent in it. Looks like I'm stuck handcuffed for another night.

"March! March! March!" I hear the voices and instinctively run to them. Where there are voices there are people, and where there are people, lies civilization. I finally have sight of another clearing, filled with hundreds of people, all lined up into rows. I creep as far to the edge of the woods as possible, in order to get a better view.

It looks to be some sort of military training camp, but they're all in uniform, all wearing the same thing. I've never seen anything like it before in my life; neither Imperians nor Obsequians wear uniforms in battle. You just wear whatever suits you.

I look around in awe at the faces before me, some of them I recognize from Imperious. They must be people—men, I only see male soldiers—who have been captured. But by whom?

And then I see him, in the first row in front of me, already looking in my direction. He is in uniform just like everyone else around him, but he does not look at the man giving them orders. He looks at me; there is no doubt about it. His line turns, putting their profiles in my direction and my heart sinks. Everything is so uniform; they've been brain washed.

It's unequivocal, every step is in unison, every turn every shift…they are all connected.

Except for one.

Because Hector looks in my direction one more time as he walks, risking his cover to do one thing. Wink. And with that wink, I smile knowing that he is just making another "round" in his personal journey.

And all that's left to worry about is who is taking care of Demi.

The only hardship on my mind.

I turn around to begin my search for a haven, moving away from the training camp when I see a pale face, a flash of emerald, and a sack thrown over my head.


I don't fight him as he carries me back to his camp. He doesn't speak to me either. I think some part of him is disappointed that I tried to run away again, but what else could he have expected?

He stops walking and then tosses me onto the ground. We must be back at his camp. "I leave you alone for five minutes…" He yanks the potato sack off of my face and I glare at him after he does. "I get it. You don't trust me." He says. Yes, there is definitely disappointment in his voice. He stands tall over me, looks at me for a second, and then moves toward the tent. "As if you'll actually respond to what I'm saying," he mumbles. I can hold onto my defiance no longer.

"You just expected me to trust you?"

He stops dead in his tracks, takes a long, deep breath, and then turns to face me. "I saved your life." He puts a strong emphasis on the last word.

"You kidnapped me." I say. "And you just assumed you'd gain my trust that way? I don't trust anyone—"

"Oh, that's right," He says, cutting me off. "You Imperians don't value life. Not even your own."

"That is a lie, you jerk! I'm a princess!"

"Yeah? And I'm a prince!" I pause and slight embarrassment registers on my face. I hadn't even recognized him in my fury. "I…"

"Save it," he says. "I don't have time to ponder with non-entities."

The sarcasm in his voice is agitating and I do not let him go. He cannot win.

"You a worthless Obsequian!" A weak attempt to pester him. He shakes his head.

"Just let it go, sweetheart." He begins to turn towards the tent again. "Take a nap or something. It's going to be a long night."

"Wait!" The word escapes me on impulse. It's my stomach speaking, not me. I haven't eaten in almost two days. He turns around in annoyance.

"What?"

"I..." I let my voice trail and he crosses his arms over his chest, raising an eyebrow. "I haven't eaten in almost two days..."

He rolls his eyes and enters the tent without a word. I can't tell if I'm more mad at myself for showing vulnerability, or for not eating earlier but I am angry, and it's not directed towards him at the moment.

A few minutes later, he comes out with a can and a spoon. I watch him as he takes a seat on the ground next to me. I stare at the can as he opens it. There are miniature noodles, "c" shaped noodles with a yellow looking sauce over them, and crumbles of something. He sets the can on the ground and starts a fire, slowly, making me wait for it.

Finally, he gets the fire going and holds the can near the fire to get it warm. "What is it?" I ask.

"Macaroni-and-cheese, an old dish commonly eaten by our ancestors. One of my favorites." He pauses and shifts the can a bit. "This is the last of it." He says the words with a slight longing in his voice, like eating this really means something to him. He pulls the can toward him and dips the spoon in it.

"If you think giving me the last of your favorite food is going to win me over somehow, you're wrong." I scowl at him again and he rolls his eyes.

"Do you want to eat or not?" He asks. I nod as I eye the food. He lifts the spoon into my mouth. It's unlike anything I've ever tasted and a part of me wants to share with him the experience, the cheesy gooeyness of the noodles with little bread crumbs sprinkled on top, but I don't.

He feeds me in silence for a while before either of us speaks. "So, you're the prince of Obsequious?" He nods his head and looks down at the ground.

"Me and my brother," he says gently. "Except I haven't a clue where he's run off to." He continues feeding me in the silence. I watch as the sun sets and I realize just how quickly this day has gone. It just sort of passed me by.

"And you're the princess of Imperious."

"Indeed I am," I say all too playfully. He turns his head and gives me a slight smile. I turn away quickly at the sight of it because he can't make my heart flutter this way.

"Last one," he says as the spoon enters my mouth for the last time. I am nowhere near full, but the meal was somewhat satisfying, so I don't ask for any more.

He stays seated next to me and looks out over the orange sky. He is sitting uncomfortably close to me, but I am incapable of moving away so I sit there, with our arms barely touching. My heart begins racing.

"Why me?"

The question shoots out of me, once again on impulse. I can't seem to control myself and my curiosity around this boy. I don't understand why, but every time I say something, it comes out differently than in the past. Nicer. I have never been so kind in my life; especially to someone who could potentially hurt me, especially to an Obsequian. "Why did you 'save' me?"

He scoots over a little bit, giving me relief and longing at the same time. He grabs a stick from the ground and draws something in the dirt between us. The sun is still high enough for me to see what it is.

It's the symbol of the Cozdle.

After he's finished drawing, he stops and looks at me. I can't read the expression on his face, as he speaks. "Do you know what this is?" he asks.

I nod my head. "It's the symbol of the Cozdle, the Cozdle Legend."

"Have you heard the legend?" he asks curiously.

"Yes," I reply softly. I cannot look away from the symbol. There's something about it...

"Did you understand the legend? Do you know what it means?"

"Um, I guess so." I allow myself to look at him again; he isn't looking at me this time, he's looking at the fire.

"So then you get that two people, two opposing and very different people, are supposed to come together to save and unite their countries." He looks at me and I return his glance with confusion.

"That's what it says?"

He nods and looks away from me again. I wonder if he's feeling what I'm feeling. "Yeah, that's what it says."

"Okay...but what does that have to do with me?"

"Can I tell you a story, Del?"

My expression does not change as I nod my head. "Sure."

He takes a deep breath and clears his throat, turns to face the fire and stares at it. The sun is just about set.

"My grandfather was an interesting man," he says slowly. "He'll always be one of my favorite people..." He stops and stares for a moment, remembering him. "Well, when I was a kid, he used to always say something to me. 'It's in the name, Cos, it's all in the name.' I never understood what it meant, always thought of him as my crazy old grandfather, always cracking jokes." He drops his head in laughter for a second and I watch him as he does so. "Man was he great…

"He told me the legend verbally as a kid but I didn't pay it much attention, didn't think it was anything other than one of his old man stories. And that is all it was at the time, for me anyways.

"At any rate, he died about six months ago, but he left me something, right before he did. Just the day before, he'd given me a box of some of his old stuff, like he knew it was his last day, like he could feel it." He pauses there, biting down on his bottom lip.

I can see how close they were, just by looking at the expression he wears on his face. "I didn't look through the box until the day after he died." He continues. "It was just a bunch of junk, a compass, a pocket watch, a piece of paper, and a leather notebook. I don't know what I was hoping for, but it wasn't in there, so I put the box away and didn't touch it again until after his funeral. And so the funeral passed and what not, my family mourned but ultimately, we moved on.

"About a month ago, I pulled the box out again. That day, I was finally ready to look at him, to think of him again and so I did. I pulled out the compass and the watch, the notebook and the paper. And I laid it all out over my desk and I looked at it. Just looked and remembered him and his scent and his stories…and then I grabbed the paper and opened it. It was a note. I must have read that note over and over again."

"What did it say?" His beating around the bush is getting to me. I don't know how much longer I can bear it. He looks at me with a gentle expression on his face, letting the words flow from his mouth like a breeze.

"The note he wrote me was practically empty. But what it said meant so much more…" He pauses again before continuing. "'Go explore, Cos. Follow yourself and explore. It's in the name'. That's it. That was all it said. And I was so frustrated, when I read it. Go explore? What the heck was I supposed to be exploring? But I still opened the notebook which had this symbol engraved in it," he pointed to the drawing in the dirt. "and inside, on the first page, was a poem. 'The Cozdle Legend'." He stops and looks at me for a second. I don't say anything, waiting for him to continue. I don't understand what he is implying.

"Have you looked at the word, Del?" I shake my head. And watch as he writes out the word close to the fire for me to see. He spells out the word as he writes the letters. "C O Z D L E," He pauses again and watches me stare at the word. "I didn't see it at first either." Cos stops and circles the first three letters. "That's my name." He states.

"Cos?"

He nods. "Yes. This is the original spelling of it."

"I still don't understand…"

"I didn't either," The inflection of his voice changes slightly as he jumps back into his story again.

"I didn't get it until a couple of weeks ago. I'd gotten that I was somehow a part of this, but what or who was 'D L E'?" He says the letters aloud again as I start to understand.

"Then finally, I looked at it. And then I said the word. And then I looked at it. And…" He re-writes the word, switching the position of the L and the E, and then underlines D E L. My name. "And then I saw it." He looks over at me and smiles a little. "And I think you do too."

I stare at the ground in awe and confusion, unsure if I believe what he is saying.

"Now my grandfather may not have been the most highly educated man," he pauses and writes it all out one more time. "But this legend has apparently been passed down verbally for generations…but somehow we fit the description perfectly."

Cos looks at me with an expectant look on his face, for what I am unsure. "That's how I knew to find you Del," he says. "Suudella Calhoun, the arrogant princess of Imperious. It's kind of hard to miss." he says with a little chuckle. I glare at him.

"You're lying," I say bluntly. The smile he wore fell from his face like a sack of bricks.

"What?" He says.

"You expect me to believe that I am apart of this legend with you? That somehow some person knew we'd be born and what not? Because if you think it's true you're crazy!"

"I don't think they knew any of this was going to happen." He says sitting up straighter. "This isn't a prophecy, it's a legend!"

"So then what?" I say. "What do you believe?"

"I believe…" His voice catches in his throat. "I believe that my grandfather saw something in me. And he saw something in you too…I'm not sure how, but he'd heard of you being heir and maybe, I don't know! Maybe he...he saw something! A-a smile or some sign and our names are merely a coincidence...I don't know." He lets his voice trail as his eyes fall to the ground. "All I know is that I trust him, with my life. And I need you on my side."

"Oh yeah," I say. "I'm definitely going to entrust my life to a boy who entrusts his to his dead grandfather. Absolutely." I say, whispering the last word.

Cos' face sets as he looks at me. And then he stands and retreats into the tent.

All I hear is the muffled shifting of his body on the ground through the lining of the tent all throughout the night.

# CHAPTER 6

When I wake up, Cos is already next to me. "If I want you to trust me," he helps me sit up and grabs my hands. "Then I have to show you I trust you," he says. I don't understand what's going on at the moment. I do not understand his tactics; I don't get how he can show so much vulnerability and then still associate with me. He tossed and turned all night because of what I said. Now I know exactly where to punch…But still he has not given up. I somewhat admire him for this as he starts untying my hands and ankles. "There," he says with satisfaction. He looks from me to my hands, and then back to me again. "I trust that you won't run away now."

I don't move. My eyes are still hazy and filled with sleep, not to mention the sun shining in my eyes. I can barely open them. But I manage to look at him, into his deep green eyes and I see something in them, but it is not distrust. For some reason, despite the end to our conversation, he trusts me. He sees something in me that is not there.

"Thank you," I say, rubbing my wrists. The wrist I hurt back at the Liable camp is even worse now, thanks to the past two days.

"Sorry about that," he says, looking down at my wrist. He takes it in his hand and runs his fingers along its sides. "I couldn't find any other way to bind you so..." I yank my arm away at the word "bind." "I didn't mean it like that," he says. "I was just..." He stops before it worsens the situation and stands again. "Look, I'm going to sleep again because last night was...rough. I'll be back later." He walks away and into the tent again, leaving me alone and free.

I sit for a while figuring out the best plot for escape. I could run into the woods again, but that probably isn't the best idea seeing that he will probably find me. In all honestly, I've never been the best at survival skills and such. I'm one of the strongest of my age, but when it comes to living on my own with a limited amount of resources, my knowledge and strength fails. Side-effect of being a princess, I guess. But I don't see any other options besides running; we are surrounded by woods in every direction. There is no other way out.

Besides killing him.

But I already don't want to do that. Not to him, he may have kidnapped me, but he has treated me well and I...

I stop myself in mid thought.

This has never happened before. I haven't not been able

to kill a person for my own benefit. And that's not going to change now. I cannot let that change now, not now, not while I am stuck in this unfamiliar clearing deep into some woods or forest or wherever he has brought me. If I want to get out, if I want my life back, he needs to be dead.

I have to kill him. It's the only way for me to escape and find out what's going on in Imperious. It's the only way for me to find out all that happened the night of the sneak attack: who is still alive, what those armies are for, what the Liables are doing.

I have to kill Cos.

The way that I have to convince myself that it is indeed the best thing to do worries me. I was trained to fight to the death, to do what ever it takes to keep myself alive. But the thought of killing Cos puts a bad feeling in the pit of my stomach, a sort of guilt I've never experienced from just a mere thought. But as I continue to think…I am not in danger. Cos has not threatened my life and some part of me doubts that he ever will. His intentions are not to kill by any means; therefore, killing him would be in cold blood…

*Stop it*, I think to myself. *You were trained for this. This is you. Wake up, Del. Do the job. End him.*

I've done it once and I will do it again. This time, successfully.

I stand as slowly as possible so as to not create commotion. My knees ache with every movement from having them bent for so long. I cannot move quickly so I will have to make his death quicker. No questions, no hesitations.

I take a deep breath and make my way into the tent. He

is sound asleep. I could crack his neck painlessly and be finished, but that would require physical contact. And I don't know the extent of his reflexes or that my mind would be able to handle that.

I tip toe around the tent as silently as possible before I spot a backpack in a corner. I walk over to it with caution and look through it, finding exactly what I need.

The gun.

I have never in my life used a gun; Imperians prefer to use more traditional weaponry: knives, swords, and clubs. But it seems this will be the only sort of weapon I will have access to, so I will take it outside and learn how to use it. Then I will come back and leave one in his skull.

And then attempt to erase the image of his dying body from my mind.

Except on my way out of the tent, I trip over his arm and awake him. He stirs long enough for me to stand and run out into the open. I am seated where I was before, gun hidden when he emerges from the tent.

"Was that you?" He asks, his voice groggy from sleep.

"Was what me?" I ask as nonchalantly as I can muster.

"Never mind," he rubs his eyes as he turns back to the tent. "I'll be up later." When he enters the tent again, I breathe a sigh of relief. My heartbeat slowly returns to a normal pace as the fear that he would catch me with his gun slowly subsides. But then he runs out of the tent again and looks right at me, dead in the eyes and I know without a doubt that he has found the gun missing. I gulp in attempt to swallow the fear and regain my confidence. I do not know why I have been acting so differently around this boy, it is as if he has stolen my morals away from me and put someone else's in their place. "Where's my gun?" He asks, slowly taking steps toward me.

I remain seated, clutching the gun behind my back, but as he begins to move quicker, I jump to my feet and cock the gun with both hands gripped tightly.

He stops moving and puts his hands above his head. "Del, what are you...I..."

"I have to kill you." I say. My voice quivers as I try to hide the slight pain I feel in the pit of my stomach.

"But I...okay." He says but his eyes do not leave mine. His jaw clenches, but the eyes do not move, they do not even falter. "I'm not letting you go. So, kill me." He gives a little shrug, his arms still in the air, his stance confident as he is now fully awake from his nap. I don't move and he cocks an eyebrow. "Do you even know how to use that?"

I pause before speaking. "No. But I can figure it out before you can take it from me." I feel my old self coming back as I speak.

"Fine," he says. "Shoot me."

I stare at the gun in my hands as I pull the trigger. I feel the cool metal under my fingers, smooth and rough all at once, move and click backward. The whole scene unravels in slow motion as nothing happens.

He is still standing in front of me. His eyes are closed, but there are no holes in him. There was no jolt of the gun, no echoing bang, his body did not stumble backward or fall forward. Nothing happened. He opens his eyes slowly and then looks to me with a blank expression on his face.

"You left the safety on," he says. "It's the lever on the back." He still does not move, but his eyes no longer meet mine. I click the safety off and hold the gun up again, but I make the mistake of looking at him, of making eye contact.

And he is looking at me. He knows. He knows I cannot do it. He knows that if I could, I would have already. There would have been no hesitation there would have been no choice. He knows that because of who I am, I would have snapped his neck a long time ago, I would have found a way. He knows that despite my best efforts, I gave him a chance to prove himself. And he has.

I slowly feel myself fade away, feel the Del I was raised to be slip out of reach. All the training lessons and survival exercises, the endless lectures on who I am and who I should be, who Imperious needs me to be: strong, trustworthy, a leader. Ruthless.

She is gone.

And I cannot kill him.

I turn the safety back on and drop the gun to my side. He approaches me slowly as tears form in my eyes. When he notices he moves a little quicker to my side. "It's okay," he says gently, placing a hand on my shoulder and prying the gun from my cold fingers. "It's okay to change."

And the tears fall forth like pouring rain.

We sit on the ground in darkness. Night as fallen and Cos and I sit by the fire. We haven't spoken, either of us, the entire day. I'm too afraid he'll yell. I betrayed his trust. He has left me un-cuffed, though he hasn't let me out of his sight. I have a feeling that he never will.

I don't like changing. I never have. Ever since I was a child, I never liked new strategies, new weapons, new people. I like continuity, the unchanging parts of life. Everything has a place and it should stay there. There is no need to go changing the way things are.

And yet here I am. Just days ago I was Suudella Iza Calhoun, heir to the throne of Imperious-- ruthless and arrogant, strong and capable. And now I'm just Del, there may not even be a kingdom left to rule and I couldn't even kill a green-eyed boy to ensure my own escape. I want myself back. Sure, I have never been the best person, sure I have never gone to church and followed the rules or listened to my parents, but I was me. I listened to Case and followed my own rules and prayed on occasion and was satisfied with that.

But now this boy.

I don't like this compassion I have for him. I don't like how easy it was for him to change the way I felt about him within a day, I don't like the way I gave up so easily on killing him. He changed me and I do not know how. I don't even know him and already he is controlling my feelings, my emotions.

I don't understand it.

I glance over at him for a second before looking away quickly. "I'm sorry," I say softly. The anticipation of his reply is unbearable.

"I trusted you."

The words sting like nothing I have felt before in my life.

"It was an impulse. I—"

"You sound like my brother," he says with a shake of his head. "And look where that got him. Lost." He stays quiet for a long moment. "Don't get lost." He says with a little smirk and I take that as his forgiveness for my mistake.

I can feel myself falling for this boy and I don't like the way it feels. I really am a different person now. The Del I was no longer exists.

"Do you have any siblings?" He asks.

"Not anymore," I say softly.

"What do you mean?"

"I used to have a younger brother," I say. "But he was killed." I let my head drop to my chest as I try to fight back tears.

"Do you know what happened?" He asks gently.

"I…I don't like to talk about it."

He scoots a little closer to me and looks out towards the woods. "That's okay."

I continue, "There was also a little girl from my country, Demi. She's like a sister to me. I found her in the Liable camp. She was brought there after me. But then you captured me. Now I don't know where she is." He looks down at me with a soft expression.

"Then we'll just have to find her, won't we?" At the word "we", my heart skips. I can feel the heat from his body against mine. We are so close together our body heat is mixing. It's making it hard for me to breathe.

"You okay?" he asks. I nod slowly.

"Yes. There are just…people."

"What kind of people?"

I wait before I answer. "New people, not from your home or mine. Liables. But they're working for someone else that's looking for something…something…" He frowns and then looks out into the night sky.

"Do you have any idea what they're looking for?" I just shake my head. He stays looking out into the sky. My mind wanders to his implications of us staying together and my breathing increases again. He is right beside me. His chin is nearly touching the top of my head and his arm is behind me. We are sitting so close…

"So, do Imperians really kiss their victims?" He asks. As he moves back, the heat between us falls.

"Oh," I laugh a little before answering. "Yeah. I mean, I kissed you…"

"Why?" He asks the question in such an odd manner it startles me.

"What?" I don't know if he's asking about my country or why I kissed him. I can't breathe…

"Why would you kiss someone you killed?"

"It's a part of our culture," I say thinking back to my home, my parents. "We kiss are victims right before they die, as they die. It's a last act of compassion."

"But why?" He asks, clearly not understanding what I have just told him. I shrug.

"I don't really know, to be completely honest. It's just tradition."

"Oh." He says. There is a slight pause before he continues. "So, when was your first one?" He presses.

I think for a moment before answering. "Most Imperians kiss their first kill. I didn't."

"Why not?"

I shake my head trying to shake off the conversation. "I just didn't. It's complicated." And then I said. "And I don't feel like talking about it."

"Then, I won't make you." And at his words, I look up at him. The fire reflects in his eyes, making them shimmer beautifully in the night air.

I don't know what this feeling is, but whatever it is I don't want it to stop. It's unlike anything I have ever felt in my life, and it is wonderful and amazing and everything else all at the same time.

I've never kissed the living, not anyone I knew was alive, at least. And I've never genuinely wanted to until now, looking at him as he looks at me. Feeling his breath on my face and his body against mine in the cool of the night.

So when he leans down toward me, I meet him half way. And I feel his lips move against mine. They are warm and soft and moist. The kiss is gentle and slow and his arm moves slowly around me as we kiss; I let a hand stroke the side of his face, feeling his smooth skin against my fingers.

We just stay there for a time, feeling each other and living in the moment. I lose sight of anything that ever was or anything that is. All I feel is him and he is all that I can think about. All I want.

He pulls away gently and looks into my eyes, our noses brushing against one another. He grabs the hand that is against his face and brings it to his lips and then sets it in my lap.

And then he pulls away completely. He moves his arm

slowly from around me, lets go of my hand and then stands. We look at each other for a long moment before he kneels and plants a kiss onto my forehead.

And then he leaves me in the dark, hopeless and wanting more, only two thoughts in my head.

I no longer know who I am.

The legend is real, and we are in control of it.

And then a third thought makes its way into my mind.

Two hearts in fear shall seek to mend.

He's scared too.

# CHAPTER 7

"I want to join you." I say the next morning as Cos walks out of the tent. He holds in his hand a small pot and has a backpack slung over his shoulder. The bag is unzipped and its contents sprawl out over the ground as he steps forward.

"I beg your pardon?" He questions. I walk over to him and pick up the fallen items, placing each one back into the sack and sealing it shut. I spent hours thinking about it last night, gazing up at the sky and realizing that this truly was the only realistic and reasonable option I had.

"I said," I repeat, "that I want to join you." He gives a light-hearted laugh before he continues.

"That's good to know sweetheart, but you were coming with me either way." I stare at him for a long moment, devising the best possible reply to his wit.

"Well," I say. "I think it'll be much easier and more beneficial to the both of us if I am willing to cooperate." We stand looking at one another as the memories of the previous night flood back to me. The feel of his lips, the warmth of his body...

"Sure thing," he says bluntly, breaking into my trance with a wink. "But for now, why don't you just sit down. I still have to pack everything up."

I am glad he does not ask me to help. I am too afraid I will find something, find out he's lying and that all of this is a scheme. Despite everything I have learned in the past and despite all of my morals, I trust him. One hundred percent.

I can't help but watch as he packs up the camp. After last night or even after the first time we kissed, back at the training facility, there has been something in the back of my mind and the bottom of my stomach. An aching or a bubbling or something that I cannot find the words to describe, a feeling, brewing there, and I have yet to figure out if I should be worried or excited.

Before I know it, he is standing before me, waiting for me to stand. I did not hear what he said, but he holds a hand out for me to grab.

I stare at it. Study it. This is the moment. This is the moment where I chose whether or not to go with him or to fight. The entire camp is packed up and on his broad back. There is no way he could beat me with all that dead weight.

I can leave, knock him out and run. I can be free. I can restore my old self and then run into the woods and back to my home. I can go back to rule my people, give them the leader they need right beside Luminary Case. We can fix this together, Case and I, and win this war, destroy the Obsequians forever. Destroy this boy and his strength, destroy his family. We have the power. I can use everything I have ever learned for this moment, finally get what I have been training and waiting for my whole life. Victory.

Or, I can take his hand. I can leave everything I have ever known, everything I have ever been taught in the seventeen years I have lived behind. I can start over. I can end the war beside him, a boy I have only known for a couple of days, a boy whose story I have never heard; the enemy…I can take his hand and turn my back to the past…recreate myself. I can let everything go, all the pain and the hatred and the sorrow. I can forget everything and move in a different direction. I can change forever.

And after a long moment of silent contemplation, after staring at his hand for what felt like an eternity, waiting to make the one decision that will change my life, I glance at his face.

And he knows. He knows I have one choice and only one: to run or to stay. He knows which one I will pick, he knows the inevitability of the situation, he knows it is impossible to avoid. He knows, without a doubt in his mind, he knows.

So, I clasp my hand into his.

My choice was made from the moment we made contact, back in the woods, at the sound of his voice…

There was no avoiding this moment.

And it's time to change.

He pulls me up off of the ground and we stand facing one

another, hands cupped together firmly. He looks into my eyes and gives a small smile before letting go and turning around.

"Well!" he says. "We had better get going if we want to make it by nightfall." He begins swiftly walking and I stumble to catch up.

"Where are we going exactly?"

"A place." He says. I frown and fall into step with him.

"Um, what place?"

"Don't worry about it." His face is hard as he says it, but it softens slowly as he prepares to speak again. We begin maneuvering throughout the tree filled woods. "Stick around long enough and maybe you'll find out." And then he turns to me and winks again.

"Is that a 'thing' in your country or something?" I ask sarcastically, drawing air quotes around me.

"Is what a thing?"

"That whole winking thing, is that some sort of ritualistic form of respect or are you just…flirting?" The last word comes out lower than I intended and he looks down at me as we walk.

He chuckles rhythmically before speaking. "Definitely flirting." And then his green eye winks one more time, just for good measure.


By dusk, we begin to slow our pace. We haven't stopped for a proper break all day and fatigue is finally getting to us. Cos isn't letting it show, but he has to be exhausted with the entire camp slumped across his back. He keeps pushing forward, moving faster with every step now and finally I can take it no longer. "Let's rest," I say.

"No," he says. "No time, we have to keep moving. We can rest when we get there."

"Cos," I say, planting my feet firmly into the moss beneath us. "We have been walking for hours. I don't think that taking a small break is going to kill us." And then under my breath, "It might actually save us."

He pulls the tent against his body and tightens his bags on his shoulders before storming up to me. "You know what will 'save' us, Del? Getting out of this forest." He pauses for a second and runs his fingers through his hair with frustration. "Do you even know where we are?"

"In the forest?" I say with a sarcastic frown.

"Yes! And the Rabid Liable Zone in particular!"

My eyebrows raise and I fidget uncomfortably, shooting a small glance over my shoulder. I've heard things about this forest. People eaten alive by Liables, flayed by Liables, dissected by Liables. Cos is right. This is not the place any person, Obsequian or Imperian, would want to be. Ever.

"That's what I thought," he says. He then turns on his heals and begins heading back in the direction we were walking in originally.

And in that moment, right as I begin to walk, right as I take my first step forward, a person comes at Cos, full speed, and hammers directly into him. He lands hard on his back, on top of the tent he has been carrying and the utter pain he feels is so visible on his face I can almost feel it for him.

Instantaneously, I flick my wrists, waiting for my Veitsen

to fall into my palms, when I realize that I haven't had them in quite some time. I lost one in my first fight with Cos and the other at the Liable camp. I am defenseless.

And as I come to this realization, the person who tackled Cos, undoubtedly a Liable, comes running at me. I dodge to the right as best I can and trip over a fallen log I had not seen. I fall hard on to the ground and the Liable, filthy and beaten, pounces on top of me and begins clawing at my skin. His nails are long and pointed and I can feel my skin ripping beneath them.

I fight back with everything I have but I am so tired and worn out that I cannot do much. The pain in my face is unbearable and I can't focus on what I have to do to get this animal off of me. I wrestle him to the best of my abilities, pushing and shoving and kicking, but he is so much stronger than me I can't get him off. Suddenly, he grips my neck with a filthy hand and leans into my face. "They're after us all! Every single one of us!" I can't breathe by now, his nails digging into my neck, his breath hot on my face, the pressure of his weight against my chest...

And then the pressure shifts as he lets go of me. The Liable is still straddling me but he is motionless. I risk opening my eyes and see hands wrapped around his neck hands that can belong to only one person: Cos.

Cos lifts the man off of me by the neck and throws him to the ground. He begins scrambling against the debris beneath him, trying to escape Cos' wrath. I have never seen him like this before. I have not seen much of him to begin with, but I have seen him fight, and the look on his face then is not what he is wearing now.

Now, in this moment, his face is pure hatred. His eyes are blazing and his face has contorted into an expression I didn't think it possible for him to wear. All of his muscles have tensed in his body and I can see a vein popping out of his neck. "Please," The Liable begins pleading. "Please don't, please don't hurt me! Please!"

"Don't hurt you?" Cos' voice flows like boiling lava. "You're asking me not to hurt you after you just knocked me over and the proceeded to choke the life out of her?" He gestures to me as he speaks.

"Please," The Liable begs. "I promise you, it won't happen again. I didn't realize! Next time—"

"Next time?" Cos asks in a low, low voice. It takes a moment and I can see his eyes watering as he bites down on his bottom lip. The Liable's eyes become enflamed as Cos straddles and leans over him slowly. Cos gathers himself, tries to get a hold of what he is about to do. "There won't be a next time." And then he raises his unsheathed sword and slits the man's throat twice over before placing the bloody blade back into its rightful place.

When he stands, he doesn't move from over the body. He stands there, staring at it for a long time and I watch him as he composes himself. I continue watching him as he makes his way over to me and holds out his scarred hand to me once more.

We make eye contact. His jaw is set and you can see the pain in his eyes as clearly as the scars on his face. Battle scars. I slowly place my hand into his and he hauls me up, letting go of me immediately after I am upright.

He walks again without a word and I follow cautiously behind him, giving him the space he seems to need. I don't understand the issue with the situation. He just did what was necessary; every Liable must die. But for some reason, this has affected him more than it should.

"Thank you," I say quietly. He stops gathering his things from his kneeling position and turns his head over his shoulder.

"Don't."

And then his head drops to his chest for a second but he shakes the emotion away and stands to face me. "We'll, uh, stay the night here. It's too dark to continue." He says with a gesture, running his fingers through his messy hair once more. He then leaves all of the camp bags piled on one another off to the side and walks deeper into the woods with his head hanging low.

That night, Cos comes back. When he sees me shivering on the ground he starts a fire and sits opposite me. The fire burns between us and I watch him through the flames, watch him as he pulls out his small sword and turns it over and over in his hand, examining the blood residue left on it.

There is something there. I don't know what it is, but there was something special about that Liable, something important enough to cause him this much pain. But I can't seem to figure it out. I try to ignore the memory, try to ignore the ruthless and evil look in his eyes...

Some part of me doesn't want to believe he is capable of that.

I don't want the myths to be true.

I stand to stretch and decide to move closer to him. I do it because I know he would probably do the same if it were me. I'm not sure what to do after, so I just sit there and watch him, watch the fire burning in the reflection of his eyes as he focuses on the weapon in hand.

"Did you know him?" I ask softly.

The look of disgust he shoots me startles me a bit and I look away. "What makes you think I knew him, Del?" His expression screams at my stupidity. I can feel it burning through my cheek.

"You seem affected. By the kill, like he was important to you."

He gave a grave chuckle before returning his attention to the sword. "Every kill is important, Del. Not everyone can do it as comfortably as you." I try not to let his words bother me and fail. "But if you must know, he was from my country. I didn't know him, but you could see the Obsequian clothing beneath the layers of cowhide. Not all Liables are born that way. Some of them choose to live that way." He looks at me again then. "He was one of those people. And now he's nothing but compost."

He stares into the fire as he had before, and I can see something I never have until this moment, how differently our worlds are, how much more personal a fight for your life can be just by being raised on the other side of a spread of land.

"But that's the war isn't it?" He says almost light-heartedly. I give a tight and uncomfortable smile, but still I am curious.

"Then why'd you do it? Why didn't you just let him go?"

"He saw us. Together. It'd have compromised our position, brought whoever these people are right to us. It had to be done." He just sits then, looking at his reflection in the hazy gloss of his sword and thinking. Remembering.

And I watch him.

During this time, this war, this era filled with hatred, it is impossible not to cry. Whether every night or every morning or every second of the day; that's just the way it is. It might not always be the result of sadness. In fact, it almost never is. Nevertheless, crying is inevitable and ubiquitous.

But never in my life have I visibly seen someone try so hard not to. Never have I watched a boy who has seen it all, death and rage and war, a boy who so personally feels the death of some stranger on his hands…I have never seen someone who has been through so much fight the tears and hold them back so well, fighting the emotions and sucking them all away, releasing them into the icy air.

But he did it. He didn't let a single tear fall as we sat there. He just stayed, concentrating on the fiery flames in front of him and the face staring back at him in the sword, ignoring my presence and the presence of his pain all at once.

I stand. I stand and walk to the pile of bags and open one of them, in search of some unidentified object, something to take his mind off of the situation. Cos doesn't seem to notice, but if he did, he does not show it. I begin looking through the bags. As I dig, my hand swipes over a piece of paper, cutting it in the process. I yank my hand back at the feeling and stick the bleeding wound into my mouth.

But curiosity gets the better of me, and I stick my hand back inside and pull the paper out. It's a picture of someone, a boy it appears, and when I bring it over to the light of the fire, I realize that it's a face I recognize.

The boy from the dock. The Obsequian I killed in cold blood.

But what was his name, what was his name...

My stomach turns at the possibilities of why Cos might possibly have a picture of this boy in his backpack as I tried to recall that night and the rise and fall of his voice as he identified himself. I gulp and lean closer to him, stick the picture in front of his face. "Who is this?"

Cos averts his eyes to the picture and then back to the fire. "That's my brother." He says passively. My heart skips in fear and I pray that it is just a boy that looks like the Obsequain from the dock and not actually him. Oh, but it is so hard to deny the resemblance.

"What was his name?" I ask much shakier than I intended. Cos looks to me, to the expression on my face that I am failing to hide, and then takes the picture from my hand. And as his mouth forms the words, I remember.

"Winton."

All I can see is the light falling from behind his eyes and the feel of his dying lips as I kissed him.

They have the same eyes...

My heart continues pounding, so much so that I think Cos can hear it. And maybe, in the dead of this silent night in the woods, he can. "Winton?"

I hate the feel of his name in my mouth, the betrayal seeping through my teeth and spilling onto him without notice.

Cos sighs. "Yeah. He stowed away on a ship not that long ago, took off in search of our long lost aunt or something."

"An aunt?"

"We don't have any remaining family besides my dad. A few months ago he told us he had a twin sister but that she disappeared some decades ago. Winton couldn't let it go. So, he took off after her. Haven't heard from him since. He chuckles to himself then. "I don't even know why I brought this. I told myself it was in case I ran into him. As if I'd need a picture to remember what my own brother looks like." And he chuckles again.

He raises his hand in order to toss the photo into the fire. I grab his hand before he can.

"Maybe you should keep it," I say, trying to disguise the feelings in my chest and keep them from showing on my face. My heart pounds faster still.

"What this old thing?" He holds the picture up. "Like I said, I don't need a picture to remember him. He can't have gotten that far. He never was good with directions."

And then he tosses the picture, his last memory of his brother, into the fire that blazes in front of us.

# CHAPTER 8

I didn't tell Cos the truth last night. I just couldn't bring myself to say the words. And the more I consider it, the more I convince myself that it is an unnecessary fact that can and should be kept a secret.

I will not tell him.

I can't.

I just can't.

The sun is rising and I am already awake. Cos stirs beside me on the ground and he rolls over to face me.

"Good morning," he says with a surprising smile. I smile back tightly, wary of his condition, and look away as he sits up, rubbing his eyes and ruffling through his hair. "We should get going," he says. "We don't have far left to go." He stands and walks over to his pile of stuff and loads it onto his back. Then he walks over to me and hands me something out of his hand.

"Here," he says. I take the object out of his hand and realize what it is immediately. It's a knife. My knife. He must have had the one I went back for the night of the battle. "You might need this," he says with a small smile: a complete turn around from the night before. "Just don't use it on me," and again he winks before turning to the dead fire and extracting the sword he tossed into it.

And for a moment I consider asking him how he is. For a moment, some sort of compassion raises out of me and I become vaguely curious about how he can go from staring blankly at his reflection in a bloodied sword to winking again. But before the words can leave my mouth, I remember my own load of guilt and decide it is better for us both if I keep all the doors to connectivity shut. Neither of us needs to share anything. Ready?" I ask him, he smiles back at me with a nod and I trot behind him into the woods and on to our destination.

"You want to tell me where we're going now?" I ask him. I struggle to keep up with him, taking two steps for every one of his long strides. "What is this 'place'?"

"Don't worry about it." He smirks a little, keeping his head faced forward. "It's not anywhere special or anything."

"Then, why can't you tell me?"

"Because," he replies. "You're a princess."

"What?" I nearly stop at his statement. "You're a prince!"

"Yeah, but, it's…different. It's…" He stops what he's saying and then shakes his head, as if that gets rid of the thought. "Never mind, don't worry about it." He speeds up his pace so

I practically have to jog to keep up with him. "Forget I said anything."

I trot beside him, failing to keep up and trying still. He is so much taller than me it almost isn't fair. I barely come up to his shoulder and he is much stronger than me without a doubt. I silently thank God for being raised in a kingdom lead by a woman, one who taught all the others how to use their agility and wit to out smart the males we so often fight. If for some reason Cos did turn on me, I could still take him. We were bred to fight the opposite.

After a while I stop glancing over at him and just run in the brush by myself. The air is filled with the scent of dew and wet leaves and provides a kind of cleansing feeling that I take in as I move, watching only the ground and hearing only the crunch of the plants beneath my boots. For a while I don't even notice him behind me. I just keep walking, unaware of our intended destination and walking still, focusing on every-thing around me instead, losing track of time and the position of the sun. But then something tells me to look over and I realize he's gone. I also realize that the trees and bushes have gone and that I am in some sort of clearing and that the sun is nearly setting.

My heart pounds in the fear of being out in the open alone and I call to him without a thought. "Cos!"

"I'm right here," he says from over my other shoulder. I can hear the amusement in his voice as he does so and refuse to turn around. He steps up to stand closely beside me, so close that our arms touch and I can feel his body heat on mine. My fingers twitch with a sudden urge to grab his hand that I fight to ignore.

"Well," he begins. "We have arrived." His voice is a cross between relief and embarrassment and I look over at him; I do not understand.

"What do you mean, 'We have arrived'? Where are we?"

"I guess you can call it our 'headquarters'…"

I see now why he didn't want to tell me where we were going. It most definitely is not special. What stands in front of us is a small house, not quite a shack, but a very small house with probably only one room. It smells like manure and salt water, likely from the lake near by. Judging from the outside of the cabin, it is going to be a very intimate and *scented* stay…

"Oh." I say and as I do, he begins walking towards it.

"Might as well get inside, right?" He calls back to me and I follow him the many yards we have left to get to the front door.

By the time I reach the entrance, Cos is already inside. I enter slowly, afraid of things I might find, cautious of unknown places given my background, title, and the war. As I make my way inside, there is a kitchen to my left, a living room and office combination to my right, and straight ahead, one bedroom and a bathroom, just as I predicted.

Somebody is going to be sleeping on the couch tonight…

Cos walks out of the back room and gestures for me to close the door. I do so and then make my way into the living room and sit down on the sofa uncomfortably. "And now," Cos says, "We rest!" He says it playfully but I do not laugh. "Okay…um, how about some food. We haven't eaten in about twenty four hours." And at his words my stomach begins to grumble. I had not realized how long I had gone without food.

Cos turns into the kitchen and begins rifling through it in search of something to make. "So," he says. "We're going to need to come up with a plan."

"A plan for what?" I ask.

He opens the refrigerator and looks over the short door. "What do you mean 'A plan for what'? Did you think I just kidnapped you and traveled beside you through the woods because you're pretty?" His eyes widen at his unintentional compliment and I feel my cheeks flush. He ducks behind the refrigerator door again. "Well," he comes out with a tray of eggs. "That is not the case." Then he turns to face me from the counter. "We have a mission to complete, remember?"

"Okay, but what is our mission exactly? So far, I haven't seen anything worth doing."

"Well, that's only because you don't want to see anything worth doing. You're lazy."

"Excuse me?" I say, offended. "Did you just call me lazy? Heir to the throne of Imperious and you are calling me lazy?"

"That," he says as he cracks a few eggs into a bowl and begins to cook. "Is exactly what I am saying."

"The nerve!"

"Oh, come on Suudella! Think about it," I look away at the sound of my full name. I haven't heard it in such a long time. "You have been pampered and catered to your whole life. You are most definitely lazy."

"You're a prince!"

"But I'm the prince of Obsequious, Del. We are raised to do the opposite. As the prince, I serve the people, not the other way around." I just shrug.

I don't admit that he is right, but he is right.

"Well," I say, "It's not my fault for being raised in Imperious. I was born there. Thankfully." I turn my nose up in the air and cross my arms over my chest. He chuckles aloud as he brings over a bowl of freshly cooked eggs for me to eat.

"Okay, Del. Whatever you say."

We eat in silence for a moment, enjoying the feeling of food in our empty stomachs. It has been too long. "So, what is this place?" I ask, finally breaking the silence.

"It was my grandfather's getaway house. He used to bring me up here all the time as a kid. When I left to come find you, I stocked this place with plenty of food and household supplies to last for a while." He pauses and looks around for a moment. "It's my getaway now."

We both finish our food around the same time and Cos collects our bowls and places them into the sink. When he turns around, he rubs his hands together like a giddy child. "Okay!" He says. "Let's get to work! What do we need...?" He walks over to the desk on the other side of the room and rifles through some of the papers. He comes back with a pad and a pen. "Where do we start?"

"You're asking me?"

He rolls his eyes and flips through the obviously used pad. "Well, yeah. I..." He pauses, looks down at the blank page for a moment and then back up at me. "Something weird is going on. I caught my father on the phone with what sounded like Luminary Case before I left. It was quiet, which was unusual. We'd all been in talks about negotiating some sort of truce and I guess he took the liberty of offering without the full consent of the Table. And then I rescued you—"

"Kidnapped," I cut in. He shoots me a look.

"I *rescued* you from that weird base camp. I hadn't even known it existed. And you said something about these new people..." He pauses again. "The point of finding you was to confirm that truce and infuse it within our own reigns. But now..."

"What?"

"I think that this may be bigger than just us."

I look at him for a moment, trying to understand. "I didn't know we were negotiating truce."

"Well, we weren't." He says. "But the Obsequious Table of Leaders had been discussing an offering. But no one believed you all would accept. My plan was to follow the ledged, find you and appeal to your senses, use our coming leadership to achieve peace. The day I left, I overheard my father accepting a meeting or something. I think that was set for the day you all attacked us on your home turf."

At that, I frown more, remembering the day of the attack and the way it panned out on our end. "You attacked us." I say matter-of-factly.

"Impossible. Obsequians don't attack. We respond."

"You expect me to believe we've initiated every battle in this forsaken war?"

"Well, yes."

"Now *that* is impossible."

"Maybe so," he responds. "But regardless, we were accepting your truce offering. Or at least the offering for discussion."

"No, no. Imperians don't 'discuss.' And besides, if something like that were underway, I'd have known about it."

"You sure about that?"

"What are you implying?" I try not to show my offense.

"I just mean…" He cautiously tries to save himself from the unintentional insult. "I know we didn't attack you all. We went to talk."

"And I know we didn't attack you. The destruction was too devastating for us to have been properly prepared. We were ambushed."

"So, then what?"

We both sit for a moment, thinking only of how two rivaling countries could both be the victim of attack in the same battle. How could this be?

And then, "Wait. What if we're missing something?" he says.

I shake my head in confusion. "Like what?"

"Like those other people you were talking about, the people I rescued you from."

"Kidnapped." He glares at me again and I let it go.

"What if," he continues. "What if…"

"They set it all up?"

And he nods. "They set it all up."

"But how?"

"That's exactly what we'd be going to find out." And I can't help but smile, not at the break through but the sheer satisfaction that shows itself on the soft lines of his face and behind the smirk he keeps trying to hide. "Looks like we have a plan!" He says and I can't help but laugh. He smiles back and my face becomes hot. "You know," he says after a moment. He faces me on the couch. I try not to meet his gaze.

"You remind me a lot of my mother."

I jerk my head towards him in amazement. "Me? How is that even possible?"

"I don't know." His gaze is thoughtful, softening by the second, and my stomach flips repeatedly as he looks at me. "She was great. Kind, obsequious, as everyone is…and you're imperious and sometimes extremely rude, ruthless. But there is something else to you that I can't quite put my finger on. Something that reminds me of her. I miss her."

I look to him again at the change of his tone. "What happened to her?"

"She died, a couple of years ago in battle. In my arms." His voice catches and I scoot closer to him, face him and look him in the eyes.

"I understand," is all I say and place my hand on top of his, gently. I cannot bring myself to speak of my parents, but I know he knows I mean it.

Without prompting he uses his hand to rub his thumb over the top of mine and looks into my eyes. And as uncomfortable and nerve wrecking as it is, I cannot bring myself to look away.

"Do you know what your name means?" He asks softly. I shake my head slowly and hold onto his hand.

"I didn't know it had a meaning."

"Well, it does." He looks up from his hand back to me. "It's Finnish, one of the dead languages. It means…" And he leans down so his lips hover over mine. "Kiss." And then his lips slowly press into them.

This was the third time. The third time my lips made contact with his. The third time I felt my heart burst in my chest and my stomach roll over and fall onto the floor. The third time that everything around me ceased to exist and the only thing I could feel was him and the only thing I wanted to know was him.

Cos.

I don't know his last name, but I know him. More than I have known any other person in the world, I know him. And I trust him.

As I relax to let the moment consume me, I am brought back to reality by the sound of distant yelling outside. It must be several hundred yards away, but I can't block it out, and the more I hear them the more I lose Cos and suddenly...

I'm pulling away. I look at his face when our lips part. It is unreadable. "What is it?" He asks.

I turn my head towards the door and listen. "Do you hear that?"

"Hear what—" And then he listens as intently as I do. I see his face change in front of me. "Yes. I do. But you're safe here. No one knows this place exists—"

"No, no. Not that. I'm not worried... That sound, the yells, unified calls and stomping. I've heard that before. When I ran away the first time in the woods and you brought me back. There was a sort of training camp." I look at him. "They sounded just like this."

He gets up then without hesitation, slings his sheath over his shoulder and tucks his gun into his waist pocket. Then he tosses me my Veitsen. "Let's go," is all he says.

I shake my head. "Wait, right now?"

"When will there be a better time?"

"Anytime after today would be a better time. Cos, anything, anyone could be out there. We don't even know who these people are or where exactly. We need to wait. Scope it out, think."

"We don't have time, Suudella. Whatever is going on out there won't wait for us. If we don't move now to see what's happening, we'll never be able to put a stop to it."

"We don't even know what it is!"

He sighs aggressively. "Look, I know 'doing stuff' maybe isn't the princess life style, but where I'm from—"

"What do you think I even do all the time?" He doesn't respond, just looks at me with his jaw clenched, conflicted.

"Suudella—"

"Save it. Let's just go," I digress. "But if we end up in a mess, remember I'll have no problem with leaving you behind."

And with that, Veitsen in hand, I walk out the door.

# CHAPTER 9

The sky is dark with heavy clouds and the smell of rain is in the air.

Cos moves closer to me and puts a guiding hand on the small of my back as we walk. I shake him off and roll my eyes "I'm sorry," he says. "It's just hard for me to believe you're more than a pampered figurehead."

"Why waste energy on such an assumption?"

"It's what we learn growing up," he whispers. "Imperians don't fight for anything but themselves, work for nothing but their own unnecessary success. I've been conditioned. And I'm sorry because I can see now that you're not actually like that."

I try to stay angry but can't help but smile at his honesty. And I can't keep from falling back into the feeling he gave me when we kissed. There's this back and forth, up and down, in and out rollercoaster with him. We're two unlike minds, forced together by some words written down by someone random out in the wilderness for hope's sake. It's a surprise we can even coexist, considering the circumstances of our introduction. And yet here we are. And here I am, falling for him.

"You aren't the only one," I say. "I've made assumptions about you too." And he smiles. "But most of mine were right." He rolls his eyes and I laugh.

"Yeah, well, that's only because I'm perfect."

"Right," I say sarcastically. "Let's go with that."

And we laugh as we walk and he puts his hand against my lower back again and I want it all to end right there. For two moments and a flickering eye I want this to be the end of any and everything and to stop and lie in the brush beside him and just exist. And for the first time I let myself feel this way, let myself think and dream and let go of my inner paranoia and edge. And I just think of him. We make no sense together and yet we somehow connect in ways I cannot even begin to define.

I think he feels it too.

And I can't help thinking that somehow it was meant to be.

Before I can get too caught in my fantasy, we come to the edge of the woods and can see the camp in front of us, filled with what looks like Liable soldiers on every end.

"How are we going to get inside? We can't pass this! What are we even looking for?" I whisper, remembering my initial frustration.

"I don't know. Anything."

"I told you this was a bad idea."

"Well, there has to be another way, a back door or something. No way a facility like this has only one entrance." I roll my eyes but nod and follow him around the edge of the woods towards a different side of the building. It's located in another clearing, this one man made. There are fences guarding it from all ends and soldiers at every entrance.

"There." Cos points ahead to a gate entrance with a single Liable pacing about. The Liable coughs and wipes his nose on the back of his hand, then looks around before retreating inside of the building probably for a nose rag. "That's our only chance." I nod again in tentative agreement and we make way to sprint across the field. This fence in particular is only a few yards away, but we don't know how soon the guard will be back. We will have to be quick.

Even though we still have absolutely no idea what we're even looking for.

"Ready?" Cos asks. I nod. "On three."

"One," I don't know what I'm doing.

"Two," I hardly know where I am. I can't do this.

"Three," And my legs begin carrying me towards the gate and through. Everything is moving so quickly and within seconds we both are on the other side. I can't keep the smile from spreading across my face at not having been caught. But when we turn around, the Liable is standing directly in front of us, his eyes wide, the tissue in his hand floating gently to the ground, weighed only by mucus.

"Newbie," I say to Cos and he nods. In no time I am on the Liable, clawing at his face and keeping him down. I flick my wrist for my Veitsen and then hold it over the Liable's head. I can feel the rage growing inside of me as the person I was merely days ago attempts to break through the wall I have put up around it. All the memories of all the battles come rushing into my mind as I take a deep breath before delivering the final blow.

"No!" I hear from over my shoulder. The knife is inches away from contact with the Liable. He lies on the ground with his eyes shut and his teeth clenched. Before I can turn around, someone pulls me off of him and drops me gently to the ground.

"What are you doing?" I say defensively. "He needs to die!" Cos just shakes his head with his eyes shut.

"No. His dead body will alarm the next people to come out here. We have to be quiet, operate under the radar for now"

Against my better judgment, I sigh and let him have this one, turning to find the Liable still seated on the ground, completely awestruck. He didn't even try to move. "Just go." And he runs in fear, after only his own safety, sprinting out of the gate and into the open.

There are no other guards around, so we walk up to the door we watched him enter and peek our heads in. Just an empty, poorly lit hallway, gray and cold. I turn around and face Cos. "Which way?"

"Left."

"Why?

"I don't know! I just picked!"

I roll my eyes and follow behind him into the hallway on the left. To our luck, there is no one in it. Cos jogs down the hallway quickly, trying to get to the other side. I follow him until something in one of the rooms catches my eye.

At the sight of it, my body freezes in place and my heart races like never before with rage. Cos stops and watches me intently as I walk up to the door's window and glance through.

Lenten.

On the other side of the window stands Lenten, the boy I once thought I'd spend the rest of my life with. The only boy to notice me, to see me, to want me. My first love and my first heartbreak, here, in a Liable camp facility.

But why? Why is he here?

Cos comes up beside me and looks through the window. "What do you see?" He looks around through the window in search of something important. He doesn't understand that this boy is what was important.

"Nothing," I say. "Just one of those traitors I mentioned." Cos nods and pulls my hand. As I begin to walk, Lenten and I make eye contact. But before the moment registers, I am out of sight.

We are in a closet.

Part of the problem with breaking into a camp with no tangible plan is once you are inside you don't know what to do. Cos found this room in search of a place to gather the information we haven't gotten.

"Okay," he says. "This was not the best idea."

"You think?" I say sarcastically and he rolls his eyes. "What are we going to do?"

"I don't know yet, I guess we could—"

"Yes, everything is in place, Sir." A voice cuts in. A squeaky voice.

"There is someone outside the door," I whisper to Cos and he nods. He listens intently as I peer through a small hole in the door.

"That's wonderful," says a different voice. This one I recognize. But from where is hard to determine…

"Also, Sir. I had this, uh, I had this idea."

"What is it, son? Can't hurt us I suppose." The second voice says. I still can't remember where I recognize it from.

"Well, I was thinking…maybe instead of picking the fight ourselves, we could set the two against each other again. Like we did last time on Imperious. That way there are fewer casualties on our end and less of them…to…fight…" His voice trails off slowly. I cannot see exactly what is happening but it seems like the lower voice has caused the first to stop speaking.

The owner of the second voice thinks for a moment. And then, "Okay. Considering they've been distanced from the rest of society for so long, they will likely fall for it again. It may work just one more time."

I suppress a gasp. They are the ones that set us all up.

"Go to the Scheduling Hall," he continues. "Set it for tomorrow if you can. Lie to them, whatever it takes, so they believe they still have to fight their way out. Because they will." And as he speaks, I begin to remember, recalling the loud, harsh sound of his voice…that is the Colonel. The Colonel is here.

"Thank you, sir!" The younger man with the squeaky voice runs down the hall on his way to "scheduling" before calling back to the Colonel. "Oh, uh, Sir? Your son is here to see you."

"Send him down." He says and on cue footsteps slide aimlessly down the hall.

"Dad," The Colonel's son's voice is soft warm and floats almost. My heart skips as I see curly brown hair through the opening in the doorway. As I watch, I can barely move.

Because Lenten is the Colonel's son.

My brain has done so many flips and turns that I don't even know what to feel anymore. Or what to believe.

"Dad, what is going on?"

"We're setting them up again. Maybe we'll get better observation this time. Ultimately, it'll help us stay under the radar with you-know-who. They want to take them down and that is easier if there are less of them to deal with as a whole. We can observe as we work towards their expansion."

"History does repeat itself…"

"Look, Lenten, I don't want to do this anymore than you do. But it's the only way we could get funding. This is not for you to worry about. You did your part, so either go back to Imperious or go home."

I peak through the hole in the door again and watch the whole scene pan out. Yes, definitely Lenten and the Colonel. And definitely related. That explains the familiarity of the Colonel upon our first introduction, and the reason Lenten, along with Tessa, was escorted inside the slave camp to meet with him.

"What is going on?" Cos whispers. I shush him and continue watching.

"Dad…"

"Lenten. I said go." So, he quietly storms away from his father.

Then another person appears and I see a blonde head nod at the Colonel.

"We need to talk." The Colonel says and the blonde nods again. I don't know if it's because of my feelings, I don't know if it's because of the pain or exhaustion or frustration, but at the sight of that blonde ponytail, I almost punch through the door.

Because that ponytail belongs to the blonde that killed my parents.

Cos can see the urge on my face and holds me back from falling through the door with hatred falling from my limbs. "Wait," he says gently.

I take a deep breath and compose myself. Then I look through the hole of the door and find that the hallway is now empty. I nod to Cos and then slowly open the door and tiptoe out of it with him on my heels.

We go left again. The voices exited to the right, and now is not the time for a confrontation. We make our way quickly down the dull, dark grey hallway to the end. I press my back against the wall and peer over the corner. There is no one in sight, so Cos and I run down the hall and back through the door we initially entered.

The Liable is gone as he was earlier, but another person takes his place.

Tessa.

She just smirks at me.

144

"Well, hello there, DelliPickle. How are you?" Her words are filled with fake happiness and I have to fight not to pounce on her, knife in hand.

"I'm great, Tess," I return dryly.

"Well isn't that just peachy?" She slowly walks forward, pulling her long blade from behind her back with every step. "So, uh, how are you taking your break up with Lenten, hmm? You still want to cry? You still think he loves you? Hmm?" She stops in front of me, turning her blade about in her hands. "Well, I see you found a rebound." She looks Cos up and down and then winks at him with a seductive smile. "Give me a call when waiting for her gets too lonely."

"Let us go, Tessa. And we won't come back."

"Oh, I know you won't be back. You know how I know?" Cos and I stay dead still. "Ask me how." No reply. She leans into my face and whispers the words softly. "Because I'm going to kill you." She begins laughing hysterically and circling us.

I flick my wrist behind my back, Cos's hand is on his sword. *Not if we kill you first*, I think to myself. She jumps towards me and sticks out her blade. I dodge it without effort. I've always been a better warrior than Tessa, always faster, always stronger, always more agile. She still hasn't realized it though and the anger on her face at her miss gives it all away.

I roundhouse kick and it hits her square in the face. She screams and throws herself at me. I am stronger than her because I do not fight with anger as my source. But I have never fought a girl before, so I am unaware of the best spots to hit

145

to win. Thankfully she is unknowledgeable of this as well, so it's a fair fight.

We roll around on the ground both trying to stab the other and failing. This fight is worthless. It will be a night of never ending wrestling.

That is, until Tessa drops her blade.

Now, I have nothing to lose.

I roll so I am on top of her, knife in hand, hovering above her exposed chest. She squirms beneath me, writhing like the serpent she is. But before I stab her, I look to Cos and see the disapproving expression on his face.

He does not want me to kill her.

Any other time, she would be long since dead, dead in seconds without hesitation. But now...

"Del?"

A voice. A heart-wrenching voice from in front of me. Tessa sees him and throws me off of her, stands beside him, holds his hand. He pulls it away and I suppress a smirk. Cos stands beside me.

"Lenten," I say. It is all I can do to keep from screaming.

I guess I did love him. "Del, what are you doing here?" He says softly. Something in him has changed.

"I could ask you the same question." I retort. He doesn't say anything right away, but the four of us stand there, facing one another.

"Look, Del. I don't know what's going on. And I don't know who this guy is."

"My name is Cos," Cos jumps in matter-of-factly.

Lenten rolls his eyes. "But I can give you five minutes before I alert the authority crew."

Cos begins pulling me as I reply. "You mean your father? The man who kidnapped me? Call them now for all I care."

"Del, let's go," says Cos.

"Wait what?" Lenten takes a step forward. "What do you mean kidnapped?"

"Lenten what are you doing?" Tessa. "Call your dad now! She even asked for it!"

"Shut up. Tessa," He continues walking forward as Cos pulls me away. "He what?"

"I guess you don't know as much as I thought you did." And then I turn and run into the woods again with Cos by my side and my heart back in my chest.

Maybe something good did come out of this.


"So, it isn't a prophecy?" I ask quietly. The night is dark and the air is cool. Cos and I are just outside the cottage with a blazing fire before us. After explaining my peculiar relationships with Lenten and Tessa, we'd remained silent, breathing softly beside each other, letting the events of the early night fade away and thanking God that the rain had not yet fallen.

"No," he says. He takes a stick from the ground and pokes at the growing fire as he avoids making eye contact with me.

This is something I have noticed about him. He is quiet, gentle, and very shy when it comes to personal situations. And that was what I had thought him to be upon our first meeting—weak. But then he killed the Liable in the woods with the purest hatred and pain and I saw another side of him, a side I did not know was there.

But watching him now, observing his very move, I realize that I do not know who this boy is at all. And some part of me is not entirely sure I can fully entrust my life with him, despite the sweet moments we have shared and his glistening smile...I cannot figure out what else is there.

"Well, if it's not a prophecy, then what is it?" I ask.

"It's a legend."

"And what's the difference?" I ask as I become agitated with his concise answers.

"It's a legend," he repeats slowly, as of I am somehow stupid for not understanding. "A story, completely made up and passed down from generation to generation for hope. That's it. Just like I said before."

"So, then how did you know to find me?" He sighs and drops the stick to the ground, stares into the flames. He still won't look at me and I'm not sure why.

"I don't know," he says. He looks down at the ground, still obviously avoiding my gaze. It is beginning to pester me. "All I know is that it isn't a prophecy. We are making it true. Yeah, sure it says a bunch of stuff. But really, anybody could have done this when you think about it."

"And our names? Is that just pure coincidence?"

He shakes his head. "I've always wondered..." he pauses for a second to gather his breath. "The first time I had even heard of the Cozdle, was from my grandfather. And you, you had never heard of it. And the few people I ever mentioned it to, they hadn't either..." he pauses again. "What if my grandfather made it up, based on us? We have no proof that any generation before ours knew of it. What if he made it up so I could continue some dream he'd always had of a united world? Or maybe something he made up just to keep me occupied so I didn't become…who they all thought I would."

At that moment, I realize who he actually is. I remember the myths.

He is the prince of Obsequious.

And I'd known that but in all the time we've spent together it never fully registered. He is the prince, son of Leader Hawse and dark heir to the Obsequian throne.

"Prince Cos of Obsequious," I say. He finally looks over at me and we lock eyes for a moment. A strong wind blows by as we are frozen in our shared trance, mesmerized by the utter presence of each other. I can see it in his eyes, I can see him in his eyes, but as I look, I become more and more unsure of what I am in search of. And then he looks away swiftly and nods his head just a tad, keeping it down afterward.

He is embarrassed. And he has every right to be. I get the feeling that he has been attempting to hide this reality from me, hoping I'd never heard.

But I have. I've heard many things about the Dark Prince of Obsequious.

In this moment, I realize that I am right to question how trustworthy he is. Because all the things he has done and the way he has treated me do not align with the stories that have been told.

He had always been different, they say. He never quite fit with the rest. Too quiet, too thoughtful, too dreamy. All of this being true. But at a young age, Cos showed his ruthlessness, and the rage that had built inside of him, killing a fellow school mate at the mere age of seven.

They said an evil brewed out of him and that they felt he would grow up to become just like Luminary Case, that somehow this Obsequian prince was more like the infamous Imperian than his own father and that he would continue the war and possibly usurp the crown by murder. There were so many things, so many stories, all ending the same way: my death or his. For I am said to be as ruthless as he, and the world has been waiting for this battle, the battle that is sure to end the war in the victory of either Imperious or Obsequious.

And yet here we are, together.

Civilized. And still alive.

The both of us.

"Everything is a lie," he says in a voice so low, I wonder if I was even intended to hear it.

"Everything? So, you would never aspire to be like Luminary Case?" He nods, indicating that I am correct. "And you would never kill your father?" Again he nods. "What about the murder on the school yard?"

And at that he remains unmoving.

"It wasn't on purpose," he says as if defending his own name for the first time, as if it has just occurred, as if he is that child again, crying to be trusted." It just sort of...happened." He looks up and over to me. "Have you ever experienced that? Fighting uncontrollably, unable to stop, entirely full of anger? And when you finally do, you think it's done and you're satisfied, you think you can forgive them and move on, you trust that everything is okay. But you realize that the person struggling beneath you is no longer struggling, the heart inside of them is no longer beating, and the life once in possession is no longer there. Because of you...even at age seven..."

I do not know what to say. I could tell him my story, tell him that I do understand and I have felt all of those feelings before. But I do not know how to react, nor do I feel comfortable sharing.

All my life, there has been only one person that I feared could ever kill me. And it was he. All the stories and rumors and tales of his hatred, of his rage, of his ruthless heart...

But here he is. Gentle and strong all at once. I have already seen him at his strongest and in his most vulnerable state. I have seen him hurt and felt his caress, felt his warmth, felt the longing in his chest when he held me to him. He has once shown me the boy I have expected for all of these years and only for my protection; no, he has treated me very differently than I was instructed.

He has shown a compassion I have seen in no other human, the sort of care I have only heard of in stories and tales of heroes.

"I am supposed to kill you now." I say. But I do not look at him. And to my surprise, he moves closer to me, leans into my side and places his hand on the ground behind me; a tease.

"Will you?" The tone of his voice, the inflection, the way he says it, the sudden change from quiet to seductive, the implication...it's as if he is asking me to rather than calling my bluff. It is an invitation instead of a fight. I cannot bear to look into his face, handsome and glowing by the fire.

But I do.

And the way the moonlight catches in his eyes and their shimmering green, the slight indication of a smirk on his perfectly pink lips, his soft breath falling against my face, I lose sight of everything; a thing that has become common for me when I am around him, this close to him. He stays unmoving for a very long time.

"No," the word slides off my tongue as a whisper, flowing from my lips to his, filling the space between us, almost as inaudible as my slowly faltering heart beat.

His smirk becomes a wide grin, spreading smoothly from one side of his face to the other as he eliminates what is left of the air between us with one of his kisses, stealing what is left of the oxygen in my lungs and sucking the life from my lips in exchange for what I refuse to call love.

# CHAPTER 10

But they are the first words to escape upon daybreak. They just fall out, involuntarily. "I love you." My eyes blink themselves open before I realize what I have said and I sit up abruptly, afraid of what he can say, trying to find the best way to cover the meaning behind such a horrid and evil phrase.

"I-I-I mean...," I begin.

But there is no response. And when I allow myself to search for his either sleeping or staring face, I find nothing.

Because he is not there.

He is gone.

But before I allow the hatred to course through the arteries of my body, I give him the benefit of the doubt.

Something I have never done before.

He is probably just in the woods, hunting or something. He did not leave me. He is fine. He did not leave me.

And at that second I hear a raging cry from the woods. I jump to my feet, checking for my knife in the process, and then take off in its direction.

In the woods, I quickly become lost in the trees. I spin in endless circles trying to locate the best possible area the scream could have come from. It's not long before I forget which direction I came from.

"I should have marked my course," I say aloud as I smack my palm to my forehead. "Stupid, stupid, stu—"

"Del!" the call comes from my right side and I take off in that direction without hesitation. The voice calling my name was not Cos', but it isn't until I'm halfway when I realize it, and isn't until I reach their location that my confidence is restored.

"Hector?" I say quietly. He smiles from the headlock Cos holds him in.

"Who else?" he says nonchalantly, as if he wasn't being held with death at bay.

"You two..." Cos stops to take a breath. "You know each other?"

I walk over to Cos with conviction and firmly place my hand on the arm that holds Hector's neck. "Let go of him," I say.

Hector stands up and Cos moves away, clearly taken aback by the situation before him. I pay him little attention though. I'm too busy looking at Hector taking in the fact that he is the first person I recognize, the first person I've seen that I am sure I can trust. He returns the eye contact with a smirk, and before I know it my arms are wrapped around him in a tight embrace.

It surprises even me, the manner in which I so easily embrace him. The way I let go of anything he could have possibly done in the time we were apart and trusted he wouldn't kill me. I knew this boy for maybe a totally of twelve hours and I have already put my faith in him. It is different. But, I think, it is okay.

"Nice to see you too, Hun," he says into my neck and I can't help but to let a shiver run down my spine. He hugs me back and lifts me from the ground. I can't help the smile on my lips from forming as he places me down and lets me go.

"How did you know I was out there?" I ask him. His smirk widens to show his unusually white teeth.

"I heard you talking to yourself," he replies with a shrug.

"But, how could you remember my voice? It's been a while, I..."

"How could I have forgotten?" he says and then begins circling around me slowly. "Miss Princess of Imperious." I can feel my cheeks burning with a fire I have only felt before with Cos and I pray it isn't visible through my caramel complexion.

"What are you even doing here?"

"Traveling," he says with a smirk. "Had some fun as a soldier. Got bored easily. You know, the usual." I laugh a little as Cos offensively clears his throat.

"So, uh...how do you guys know each other?" He says.

"Well," I begin. "Before you decided to kidnap me from the Liable camp, Hector was my...cage neighbor, if you will." Hector sticks out his hand to Cos for a shake. Cos looks from it to Hector, to me, and then back to the hand before not taking it. Hector puts his hand down.

Cos averts his attention to me. "We need to go." I look at him for a long time, almost annoyed at his uncomfort.

"Okay, fine. We can go," I say. "But Hector is coming with us."

Cos' gaze remains on my face, solid aside from his clenching jaw. "Del, I don't—"

"Cos!" I yell. And then I walk up to him with more confidence than I've had in the past couple of days. "He is coming." He looks down at me, returning my plain and firm expression before turning slowly on his heels and beginning to walk.

"Well isn't he just a big ball of fun," Hector says to me under his breath as we walk.

"Shut up," I say with a small grin and we both laugh.

"But seriously, how did you even find this guy?" he asks.

"He found me," I reply.

And our conversation ends there.


At the cabin, Cos talks very little. He moves around swiftly, serving Hector and me simply because it is in his blood. He cooks, he cleans, and then finally, after an abundance of time, he sits. Not near me, and not near Hector. Alone in a chair across the room, he finally feeds himself, plays music in the music player his grandfather left behind to drown us out.

Hector pays him little attention and the two of us talk as Cos isolates himself. But I can't help but watch him simultaneously. I can't help but notice the way he looks at us from the corner of his eye, can't get past the expression on his face.

He looks like a lost child.

As I am about to stand and go talk to him, Hector senses it and latches onto my arm.

"You can't trust him," he says firmly, looking into my eyes.

"What do you mean?" I ask skeptically, curious as to what he already knows.

"I mean, while you were in the bathroom, before he started cooking, he received a phone call."

"A what?"

Hector is talking very quietly, and out of the corner of my eyes, I see Cos watching us, but the music is still playing in his ears, so he can't hear.

"A phone call."

"And what did he say?"

Hector hesitates before speaking. "He said—"

"Okay. We need to plan this." Cos says. My heart jumps and my stomach lurches as my mind registers the convenience of his interruption.

Maybe he could hear.

And maybe he doesn't want me to know about the phone call.

He is hiding something from me.

Cos notices my troubled expression and looks at me for such a short amount of time, my fears increase. He sits across from me and I refrain from moving closer to Hector.

"So," He says. "There is some battle possibly set for to-morrow…"

"Yeah, they confirmed it." Hector says. Cos and I simultaneously look at him.

"Wait, how do you know that?" I ask him.

"I was one of the guards at that facility. They used to talk about stuff like this a lot. Then I got bored with it, ran into the woods, almost got killed by this guy," he gestures to Cos. "And then found you," I look away, suppressing a surfacing smile.

"That's funny because they just decided on the battle while Del and I were there." Cos says, confused by Hector's knowledge of what's going on. Hector remains silent for a short second before replying.

"Well, they've been wanting to 'expand' whatever that means. I guess they're narrowing down the crowd." Cos nods with a slight glare in his eyes that openly says exactly how he's feeling. He does not believe a word out of Hector's mouth.

"Well then, Mr. Know-It-All," Says Cos. "Where do you think they might hold something like this?"

Hector points away from the facility we all came from, in the opposite direction. "That way. Towards the beach."

Cos leans forward skeptically. "Why so close by?"

"These people aren't very big on traveling far distances.

"And why should we trust you? You did, after all, show up right after we came out practically. How do I know this isn't a set up?"

"I'll go with you," Hector says confidently. He is not at all shaken by Cos' accusations.

Cos slowly leans back with his arms crossed before surprising not only Hector, but also me. "Fine then," he says. "Since you know tomorrow is for sure, it's worth a shot." He stands and walks toward the small hallway, leading to the rooms of this cabin-like house.

"Wait," Hector says, standing. "Just like that? You're just going to go? After all of that, you're just going to trust me?"

"Yes. Why? Should I not trust you?"

"No, it's just...shouldn't we talk it out, maybe? Devise an actual plan? I don't know about you, but I am not about to get myself killed."

Cos shakes his head. "Not necessary. We'll be fine."

"Who put you in charge, bub?" Hector presses.

"My birth right." Cos has become defensive. I almost visibly see the brick wall that now surrounds him rise up.

They are about to fight, and I can see it. And I can't let it happen. I grab Hector and make him sit back down. Then I stand and make my way over to Cos.

"Okay, so we're going. But, what are we even going to do?"

"Well, what other choice do we even have? We're going to talk to them."


Hector is sleeping on the couch.

Cos is in the back room.

I am in the bathroom.

I feel sick. Sick with emotion, sick with frustration, sick of it all. There is too much swirling around my head and I feel like I am going to throw up everything inside of me. I can almost feel my dinner creeping its way back up my throat.

I don't know what to do...

"Hello?" Cos' voice from outside the door.

"Yes, I'm—" I begin. But he cuts me off.

"No, no. That can't be right. It's not…"

He's not talking to me.

"Yes, she's here…No, she's sleep."

And he doesn't know I'm in here. I get the feeling I am not supposed to be hearing this conversation.

"Yes, with the other one…of course not! Do you think I'm stupid?"

I walk slowly to the bathroom door and crack it open, peaking through the slit. He is on the phone, his back to me. My heart pounds.

"No, they have no idea. Well, he does, but I stopped him before he could tell her…I know…I know!…I know. Okay! Look, he'll be gone by tomorrow. Don't worry," He peers around, making sure he's not being watched. He does a poor job. "I'm not going to screw this up." And then he hangs up the receiver and walks back into the back room.

As soon as he's gone, I creep out as quietly as possible.

"How long were you in there?" His voice is loud to me although it is merely a whisper. I nearly jump out of my skin at the sound of it. I turn around slowly to face him. His face is stern.

"What?"

"How long were you in there?" He repeats.

"I just went in. For a tissue." I lie. "Why?"

But he just turns and walks deeper into the room.

He knows.

And so do I.

A few minutes later, I find myself at the beach alone. It's not far and I need the salty air, to clear my head, to assess.

Cos is lying to me. He is using me for something, trying to get me somewhere, alone. And he is going to get rid of Hector. He'll probably get rid of me too eventually. This is all probably just some well-devised scheme to kill me.

Take care of me.

Pretend we're a team.

Make me fall in love.

And then deliver the final blow.

They always said love is the greatest weapon…

It takes a second before I realize that I just admit to myself that I am in love with him. But, then I think about Hector and the way he makes me blush and the way I feel like gelatin when he smiles.

Is it possible to love two boys at once?

I've never believed such things possible, especially so quickly. A week ago I barely believed it possible to love just one. But when I think back to the moments I've had with Hector and then think about the few days I have spent with Cos… it is hard to gainsay the feelings I have for the both of them. But reality is already pointing in one direction…

Just then, footsteps stop behind me on the sand. I'm not startled. I know it's Cos. I've practically been waiting for his arrival.

So when he says, "Del, are you okay?" I don't move and simply wait for him to sit beside me. He does. "What's the matter?" He asks.

I shrug. I cannot even begin to put my feelings into words.

"Well, whatever I did, I'm sorry. Whatever I said, I didn't mean. Del, I think I—"

"You were on the phone," I say cutting him off. I look over at him and he looks away, fiddles with the sand between his legs.

"Yes. I was on the phone," he says.

"With who?"

"That doesn't matter…"

"With who?" My voice becomes more firm. I feel my eyes go cold and his expression wavers before he looks away again.

"Someone from Obsequious tracked me down to tell me that they found my brother."

I know he isn't telling the whole truth. I don't know what he talked about earlier, but I know just now, he was talking about Hector and me.

"They found you?"

He nods.

"Do they know I'm here?"

"They haven't the slightest clue. They think it's just me." He says with a self-deprecating smile. "All alone, Prince Cos of Obsequious. As usual." He chuckles to himself but I stay staring at the ground in front of me. I hold my arms to myself, less cold from the wind and more from his lies.

"You cold? You know, I don't know what it is, but I…I just wanted to tell you that I—"

"Why are you lying to me?" He sets the arm he was about to put across my shoulders down.

"What are you talking about?"

"Why are you lying? You're lying to me." My eyes are watery from the aching I feel from sitting next to him.

"I'm not…"

"Of course not." I pause for a moment. Deciding whether or not I will confront him or let it go.

I fail to be humane.

But I succeed at being human.

"Did you get rid of Hector yet, Cos? Did you do what they asked of you?"

His eyes widen as we make eye contact and then he looks at the ground again. He is too weak to even look at me. "You said you were getting tissue." His voice is quiet beneath the waves of the ocean before us. "You lied."

"Yes, Cos, I lied to you. To protect myself."

"Well, then that makes you as bad as me!" He stands and looks down at me. "How are you any better?"

"Don't try to flip this on me, Cos. You know what you did is worse!" I stand and face him. "You're in contact with your country! How do you expect me to trust you?"

"Well maybe that's why I didn't tell you, Del. Because I want you to trust me!"

"But why? Why don't you just kill me now?" We are yelling by now. We are screaming the words at one another, spitting them.

"Because I need you! Because they just told me they found my brother's body, washed up along shore, dead! Because you're the only person I trust with my heart, Del. Because I love you!"

There is silence among us. The only sound to be heard is

the waves of the ocean beside us, the gentle crashing as they make contact with the sand and then slowly recede back into the watery hole.

He wants that to fix everything.

He wants those words to ring in my ears.

He wants me to hold him then, stroke his quivering face.

But I cannot stop the words from spilling out of my mouth. Maybe to hurt him, or maybe to get it off of my chest, I am not sure. But they spill like flowing water.

"I killed him, Cos." He lifts his head from his chest, every emotion possible, visible in his glossy eyes.

"What?"

"I killed you're brother Cos!" It is anger. To him, it is anger toward him. But to me, it is anger toward myself. To me, I am screaming at my own choices. But to him it is different. "He was in our territory, and you know what I did? I stabbed him in the gut and twisted the knife inside of him twice. And I promise you, I kissed him. And I swear above he died a slow and very painful death."

I await the blow for a very long time. But he just stands there, looking at me, searching my every move. I can read the hope on his face, I can see that he prays with everything inside of him that I am lying.

But I'm not.

Silently, my words continue to register in my own mind and I feel an abundance of sympathy towards him. I cannot trust even my own self.

"Winton was his name, wasn't it? He seemed like a good kid," I say. "But, I am not."

# CHAPTER 11

The sun shines brightly through my eyelids the next morning.

I slept on the beach. Cos ran off after I told him the truth, after the truth flung from my lips, and so I stayed behind at the beach giving him the time he needs to recover.

The truth needed to come out, but not like that. Not when he was being so kind, not when he was trying to keep me warm, not when he was expressing his true feelings, not when he had just told me...

Not when he had just told me he loved me.

I've never been loved before. I don't believe I remember ever hearing the words from my parents properly, I never really had any friends, and Lenten...that wasn't love.

That wasn't even close to love.

But Cos let his guard down. He broke through his wall and told me that he loved me. He let himself become vulnerable and I stabbed him the first chance I got.

And what is worse is that I can't tell whether what I said was deliberate or not. Whether it was coming before he'd said it, or came out as a reaction to what he said.

I've never felt remorse before.

But I have a feeling that this is it.

I stand and brush the sand off of my clothes and skin, stretch and walk toward the woods. Whether any of us likes it or not, we're fighting today. We're changing today. Everything is changing today.

I stand in front of the door and take a deep breath before walking inside of the cabin. When I do, Hector is eating on the couch, but Cos is nowhere to be found.

"That's your plate on the table," Hector says with a mouth full of food. "And he's in the back room." He pauses and hesitates. "In case you were wondering."

I nod once and then sit at the table, staring at the plate of food. "Did he make this?" I ask, turning to face Hector in my chair. He nods and then I face my food again.

I don't for a second believe he would poison me. I want to believe that, but I don't. I wish he had, though. I hope he has. I hope he has the hatred to end me. I hope I pay for what I did to him. And I hope he's the one to do it.

But he's not like that. He's been through too much to change now, to kill me on the spot. Despite what I deserve.

I eat what I can, forcing food down my throat. But the more I eat, the sicker I get and before I know it, I am running back to the bathroom.

I throw up from food, remorse, self-hatred, and tears. The

waste won't stop coming and the tears won't stop spilling off of my face. When finally, my stomach has disposed of everything it needs too, I sit upon the floor and let silent tears fall onto the tiled floor. It doesn't feel like crying, but it is. All I want is for him, for Cos, to come in and hold me, to tell me he forgives me, that he still loves me, and that everything will be okay, that we are in this together, that nothing will change, that he'll never let me go.

But he is not who comes. Hector is. He comes in and closes the door behind him before flushing the toilet I threw up in and picking me up off of the ground. He stands me up and then wraps his firm arms around me and I stare into his shoulder.

I don't know what I've done. I have made a lot of mistakes in my lifetime, and I have killed a lot of people. But this is somehow so much different, this somehow means so much more than anything in the world. And there is no way for me to fix it. There is nothing left for me to do but let my sob-less tears soil my friends shirt.

I have changed.

Completely and utterly different from the girl I was because I somehow now need other people. I have never needed anything from anyone in my life. And yet, here I stand. And only because another person helped me up from the ground.

"You're the only person I can trust," I say between tears. He presses his lips to the top of my head and sways from side to side.

"I know," he replies.

And in that moment we hear a raging Cos.

"I have got it all under control!...No, you aren't hearing me, she knows things now. Because of you, everything is ruined!...Yes, I am aware of that...Another?...Who?...Okay, I'll fix it and then

I'll figure it out…Alright. I'll find her. And then I'll end her."

I pull away from Hector slowly. We both look at each other with stricken expressions.

Cos cannot be trusted. He has made that very clear in the last twenty-four hours. I don't know who he is working with, or what he is hiding, but it is something much greater than I could even imagine.

Hector and I come out of the bathroom together, a newly formed team. But, as soon as the door opens, Cos walks out of the back room. As he sees us standing there together, his jaw sets and then he continues down the small hallway. My breathing is rugged.

I am at an utter loss.

"We have to go." Cos says. He doesn't wait for us as he walks out the door.

Hector squeezes my hand before we grab our weapons and step out into the open.

We stay concealed within the trees as we wait for each opposing side to arrive.

I don't know what to expect. None of us do. But this is going to be an extremely bloody and death filled event. I'll be surprised if anyone makes it out alive. Including us.

But, according to the Colonel, that's what they want.

Cos decided we would wait. We would let the fight begin and take in what we can, try to figure out what it is that they're looking for, what this is really about. And then, we would move in, stop the fighting and talk to them, get them on our side.

Imperious and Obsequious together.

"This isn't going to work," Hector says. "This makes no sense what-so-ever. You want both sides to be all buddy-buddy by the end of this? You're crazy, man, c-r-a-z-y..." I smile at Hector, how he spelled out the word. He is quite intelligent for a simple traveler.

"Just go with it, okay?"

"This isn't going to work, man..." As his voice trails, we all see the first people to arrive. Obsequians. I cannot help the scowl that appears at the sight of them.

Conservative clothing, completely covered. Bright, happy colors. How can warriors wear clothes with such an implication of happiness?

Contradictory.

Not long after, the Imperians arrive, half clothed and dark, characteristic of our country. The less the clothing, the less chance you have of being pulled back by your shirt.

We wait silently within the brush, watching intently. We cannot hear a thing, but we do not need to. The designated lead of each side steps forward, a woman from Imperious and a man from Obsequious. They stand very close together, speak, and then suddenly her blade is out and in his chest. He falls to the ground and she leans over and kisses him as we Imperians do. Then she looks over her shoulder at her people, looks ahead of her at the enemy and the screams, a gesture of beginning on Imperious.

The Imperians charge the Obsequians who stand waiting, never initiating, only retaliating. That is how they fight, they wait until they are attacked first and then jump right in, weapons and all, only attacking in situations of the protection of someone else.

And thus the battle begins.

But I pay little attention past the kiss between leaders. Because I noticed something. I've never really watched one occur this way, let alone at all. We're all too focused on fighting to win. But there was a heaving of the man's chest as she kissed him, as if he was breathing something into her, giving something away.

I do not say anything, but I notice and take a mental note of it for later.

"So, what are we going to do?" I ask.

Cos answers matter-of-factly. "I'm looking for the people that set this up. They won't stay forever, if they cam at all. So, when they bail, we jump in." He makes the mistake of looking at me and I can see his chest heave.

"Cos, I'm—"

"Not now, Del." He looks at me intently. "Not now."

Hector looks at me from the corner of his eye and I try to avoid his gaze. I know he doesn't trust Cos. And I'm not so sure how much I trust him either.

"Look!" Cos says. "Right there, in the lake, straight ahead." Hector and I look to where his finger points. "It must be a submarine camera sort of thing. That's where they're watching from."

"So, now what?"

Cos waits before replying. "We wait." We don't want to be seen on that camera."

I nod. "Hey, Hector?" I begin. But when I look over, I realize he is no longer there. "Hector?" He is nowhere to be found. "He's gone..." Cos looks to me for a small second before looking away.

"We need to focus..."

But that is all I hear. I can't breathe. He left. The only person I know I can trust left. Left me with someone who very well may be out to get me. I have never felt so alone before in my life. This is why I have always chosen to not love and to stay alone. You don't feel alone when it is a choice.

I look up at Cos again, who pays me no attention. He is looking at something to his left though, and I follow his gaze to an old man dressed in a very white suit. Suddenly anger and fear boil within me simultaneously.

That must be the man he's working for.

There isn't a doubt in my mind…

"Now!" Cos, yells. And without thought, I follow closely behind him out into the open sand. Instantly we are included in the fight, a fellow Imperian attacking me before seeing my face. They quickly back off when they do.

The Obsequians slowly break off upon seeing Cos. They stop and close their eyes. Some sort of unified respect. And many of them die because of this. I scream as signal for the Imperians to stop before any more of them are brutally killed.

Everything stops.

The only noise is from the lake. I look out into it and see that the watching device is indeed gone. Cos and I will not get caught so long as it does not return.

The pack of people slowly forms into a circle, confused faces surrounding, all asking the same questions: Why are they together? And why do they want us to stop?

I could ask myself the same.

I take a deep breath before beginning. Cos remains silent and I say the first words that come to mind; the first idea in my head.

"Just stop for a second. Stop fighting, stop hating…just stop." I pause and take another deep breath before continuing. "We are all fighting for the wrong reasons and now there is someone out there taking advantage of that purposeless hatred."

"This is bigger than just us now," Cos continues. "And we can't fight back without you all on our side."

"Together as one country, one world," I say

And then Cos and I, at the same time, as if rehearsed, "United."

Nobody speaks. Nobody moves. Cos and I stand in the center of the ceased battle as we await a response.

But in the end, we have to leave, fight our way out. In the end we are ignored, pushed aside and discarded. We do what we can to escape the bloodbath and once again reach the woods, our only safety.

I almost didn't notice the Colonel.

I almost didn't see the man in the white suit on the other side.

And I almost didn't see the disapproving expression of Luminary Case in the distance.

But I did.

# PART III

# CHAPTER 12

It's just past midnight.

Cos and I have been sitting in the cabin all day in silence.

It didn't work. None of it did.

And it makes sense why it didn't. I mean, how in the world could Cos and I both decide, with no prior consent, that we would try to bring our countries together? Just on a whim?

So, of course it failed.

And what is eating me is the fact that I actually believed, without Cos' convincing, that we could actually somehow change their minds.

Hector disappeared. I haven't the slightest clue where he ran off to. So, in addition to the sudden loss as for what to do, I'm worried about him. I fear for him.

And then there's me alone with Cos.

Who knows what's going on there.

He sighs dramatically. "What are we doing?" I stay quiet and let him vent. "I mean, what were we thinking? No...we weren't even thinking!"

He does not mention the man in the white suit.

I don't say anything. I just watch him as he paces back and forth, repeating himself over and over again.

I just watch. I don't know what to say. And I know whatever I say, no matter what the words actually are, will remind him that I'm the psychopath that killed his brother.

And that is how he will forever see me.

"And! He says for the umpteenth time. "Hector is gone! He could be anywhere and with anyone!" He stops directly in front of the armchair I sit in and leans into it, his face very close to mine. "He knows this location. He could bring someone here...oh man, oh man, oh man..."

"So, what do you want to—"

"I'm back!" The door to the cabin opens and slams shut as Hector makes his way inside singing the words. "Where were you guys?" He begins, "I went to go check out the area behind us, thought I heard something in the under brush. And when I came back, you guys were gone!"

Cos and I stay staring at him from our close position. Slowly, Cos turns his head to face me. He looks into my eyes and I can tell he thinks this confirms all his suspicions.

While he continues to confirm mine.

"Did you find what you were looking for?" Cos asks skeptically.

"Nah," Hector replies. "Must have been a little critter or rodent or something like that." Cos nods once.

"Well, I'm glad you're okay…" Cos' voice trails. Hector squints his eyes at him before coming and sitting on one of the arms of my chair, draping one of his own arms across my shoulders, leaning down and kissing my forehead.

"So, what is plan D?"

"We don't have one yet," I say. Hector looks taken aback.

"You don't have one? It's nearly been twenty-four hours and you don't have one?" Cos avoids eye contact. "Well, lucky for you, I just might."

"What have you got?" Cos becomes intrigued and sits upon the coffee table in front of Hector and me.

"Well, I wandered along the coast for…quite sometime trying to find which direction the cabin was actually in, and in doing so, I noticed this enormous facility down the way. Then I realized it wasn't just any facility, but the Obsequious castle."

I look to Cos who keeps his head down. I was not fully aware of how close to his home we actually were. More and more secrets, more and more lies…

"But as I got closer," Hector continues. "I noticed that some iffy stuff was going on and that the guards weren't Obsequian guards but Liables."

Cos looks up intently. "Liable guards? In my castle? The one I live in?" Hector nods. "How is that even…"

"Looks like they found a way inside and took over. So, that's where we need to go."

Cos nods and I look from one boy to the other, unwilling to speak for fear that I will somehow ruin this unspoken truce they have unintentionally created.

"So, when should we go?" Cos asks.

"Best time to leave in my opinion would be morning. That way, we get there by nightfall and can infiltrate in the dark."

Cos nods and gets up from the table. "I guess that means we should get some sleep, eh?" We could use the rest." He's looking at me when he says it so I nod and he then walks away to the back room.

"He's right, Del." Hector says. "Get some sleep." And then, in the most peculiar tone of voice, "You're going to need it."

I find it somewhat odd that I am somehow able to sleep that night. We actually got away with stopping the fight and talking to the people, despite all the watching eyes. We actually have a plan to infiltrate the royal palace of Obsequious. We might actually be capable of getting what we want...

In the morning, Cos comes from the back room and sits down beside me on the sofa. I sit up as he takes a long, deep breath and looks at me with a firm expression. It doesn't quite look like he slept as well as I did.

"We have to leave him," he says. I frown at him and shake my head.

"What are you talking about?"

"Do you really believe that story, Del? That he was just walking around and just so happened to encounter the palace? That he got lost and didn't deliberately leave?"

"Yes, Cos," I stand and face him. "I do believe him."

Cos stands up abruptly. "But how can you?" He stops himself and looks over his shoulder, quiets his voice. "How can you look at his serpentine face and trust it?"

"Because he's not the serpent, Cos."

"This is bigger than that, Del!" Cos is nearly yelling. He quickly changes his tone of voice and bends down, talking directly into my face. "And you have no right to be angry at me, okay? I didn't kill your brother!"

"You're right! I did!" The words slip from my mouth before I have a chance to catch them.

That catches him, but he recovers quickly. "What? Look, just, stop putting things into my head and listen to me! I have put my anger towards you aside so we can finish this." He puts his hands on my shoulders. We are standing very close... "You can't trust him, Del. He's making this too easy for us, there is something—"

"Stop." I don't yell, I don't scream, I just say it. Cos looks at me and takes his hands from my shoulders. "I will trust whoever I want to trust. And right about now, it isn't you. Midnight phone calls and 'finishing her' don't really strike me as the sort of thing I want coming from the person backing me up."

Hector comes out at that moment, giddy and excited for the coming adventure. "Well, you guys ready to hit the trees?" I can't help but to laugh at his horrible joke and I walk over and link my arm with his. Cos watches us from across the room and just as we are about to make our way to the door, gunfire pours in.

"Get down!" Cos yells. He and I both hit the ground like never before, but Hector stands, stunned by the situation. I yank his pant leg.

"Hector! Get down! You're going to get—"

But before I can even finish, Hector topples onto me, a

pile of dead weight.

He has been hit.

He looks at me through a coming haze and manages a smirk before going completely limp.

"Hector?" I say. "Hector!" I can't control the barrage of tears that attacks me, can't control the empty feeling in my chest.

This is why I don't love.

They all die.

Cos crawls over to me. "Shh! They can hear you!" He tries to put an arm around me to tame my emotional convulsions but I fight him off.

"Don't touch me!"

The door opens.

Cos only manages to whisper in my ear, "Play dead," and pushes me to the floor.

I hear boots on shards of glass and wood walking slowly into the cabin. I close my eyes and ignore the life around me.

I am already dead. I haven't one reason left for living now. Hector was my last one…

Almost as quickly as I gave up, my mind wanders to Demi. Little more than a reflection of my younger self, she is all I have left now. And upon remembering that, I hold my breath and keep my eyes shut. When one of the men kicks me, I roll over as limply as possible. He has to believe I am dead in order for me to find and save her. If that is even still a possibility.

Finally, they stop observing us. I open my eyes to slits. I see the Colonel and a blonde ponytail.

"Should we take the boy?" The colonel says.

"If we take him we can use his body against Hawse." Another voice, this one female. "But knowing my brother that would send him right into the frenzy he needs to win. We can leave him here. Hawse can come find him after he surrenders."

"And the girl?"

"Leave her too. Her parents are already dead. She was never strong enough anyways. Not worth keeping."

Neither of them acknowledge the third body.

It takes everything I have not to move, every ounce of strength left to stay there, almost dead.

Because the unmistakable, raspy voice of long time ruler of Imperious keeps ringing in my ears.

I watch motionlessly as Luminary Case saunters out of the cabin behind the Colonel, comfortable in yet another victory.

It was her.


When they are finally gone, Cos and I sit up. Both covered in the blood of Hector, but neither with our own wounds, thankfully.

I look over at the dead body.

"Is he really dead?" I ask quietly as I scoot myself closer to him and place a hand onto his back. Cos reaches out a hand and places two fingers to Hector's neck. His movement is lethargic and I can only imagine what might be weighing him down.

"No pulse."

I just nod.

Cos sits beside me and neither of us move, me shaken not just by the dead Hector but the knowledge of my parents' killer and Cos aware of only one thing in the now worn down cabin.

His father's long lost twin.

His biological aunt.

The ruler of Imperious.

My mentor.

My parents' murderer.

Luminary Case.

So, we sit there, taken by the moments as they pass, stuck in a lapse of confusion and uncertainty, drowning in the depth of our current experience.

This might be the end.

With what little strength we had after hours in the scattered glass and wood of the cabin, Cos and I made it out and back into the woods.

We left the body.

Neither of us could bring ourselves to touch it. It was just too much for the both of us. We considered burning the body, but it was a lot for me to handle and a lot for Cos to handle and neither of us could quite put the pieces we needed together in order to move forward.

We didn't see it coming.

There was no way for either of us to have known we were being followed, or that the one person I trusted would be killed in front of us, or that my mentor killed my parents, or that Cos's aunt was the leader of the country he grew up loathing and that I killed his brother while he was looking for her, in search of family. Neither of us saw any of it coming.

Neither Cos or I speak on the way to Obsequious either. I cannot stop myself from reliving everything over and over again. Neither can he. And neither of us knows how to help the other.

"I didn't think she really existed," he finally says.

"She killed my parents," I respond.

"It almost makes sense now. Why I..." He looks at me, stricken and guilty, like her actions were somehow a reflection of him. "I'm just like her. It's...it's in my blood."

And I want to say that he's wrong, I want to tell him not to believe that, that the man he has molded himself into is the man that he truly is, but I don't. I just look away.

He lets out a hefty sigh and keeps walking.

Regardless of our newly formed bond over the betrayal and hatred imposed on us by one common link, Cos and I are distant. That is the only conversation we have on the way to his castle, the only thing we can even think of to talk about. Too much has happened for things to even remotely revert back to the way they were.

So, I am back to where I started.

Alone by will.

Alone by choice.

Alone by force.

These are all the reasons why I do not ever let myself go and why I do not let my guard down. I am walking with an Obsequian, a servile weakling and an enemy of my country. I let myself fall for an Obsequian, I let myself open up to an Obsequian. I let myself change for an Obsequian. And it wasn't for the better.

I almost lost my life.

If I had run when I'd had the chance…

"Okay," Cos speaks again as we near our destination. "We are almost there. But let's take a rest break. We're going to need to—"

"They saw us," The words fall out of my mouth before I can stop them. "At the battle they arranged." He riffles through his knapsack. "I saw them. And I guess they saw us too."

"Yeah, I know," he responds. I am surprised.

"You know?"

"I also saw them there." He nonchalantly takes a swig of water, then hands me the bottle. "We lead them right to us."

Neither of us knows how to respond after that.

We just didn't try hard enough. "We should keep going," I try. It's better when we're walking, less uncomfortable.

"No, I really think we need to rest for a bit before we continue. We can't be tired once we get there."

"I don't think I can wait any longer, Cos. We've already ruined this once. Let's just go."

He sighs. "Del, I really think—"

"Please."

He puts the water away and stands.

"Okay," is all he says.

It's too easy.

We got to the gates and they were open.

Lights were on but no one was around.

No guards.

No civilians.

Nobody.

"Cos,"

"Shh!" He says.

"Cos, this is…"

"This is what?"

"Easy."

We are pressed against a wall side by side. It is a dark night only illuminated by the full moon and small lights within the royal palace.

Cos looks down at me and purses his lips before nodding slightly. "Yeah, I know." He pauses and looks over the edge of the wall. "I have a feeling we could walk through the entire palace in the open without getting caught."

"Then why don't we?" I say. He frowns. "If we know they are waiting, why not show them that? Why not walk in with confidence?"

"You mean *imperiousness*?" he asks with a smirk, and I nod with a small smile. And for just that moment, things felt normal again. For that moment. And then, "Let's do it."

And so we both step out into the open together, aware that we are being watched, but imperious all the same. Cos let's his supressed arrogance show and I almost laugh.

This is why I liked him. Because of his sense of humor, because of his kind heart, because of the person he is on the inside, the person that I got to know.

But I can't help questioning, can't help doubting, can't help feeling…

Maybe this is still all on him, all his fault, maybe this is all still apart of his plan.

Just maybe…

The main palace's doors await our touch as we stand in front of them. Cos and I look to each other before each placing a hand on a door and pushing our way inside.

Upon entering, we are wafted by blinding, bright light. And, just as we suspected, everything is there. We were right; they were waiting. Plotting.

"Del!" I hear. I look to my left and see little Demi, locked in a cage. She is accompanied by a large middle-aged man, with a balding head.

"Cos," he says.

"Dad?"

"Ah, I see you've found our insurance," a voice says from across the room. Within seconds, our wrists are bound and held by guards in black and red. They push us forward and onto our knees before the Obsequian throne.

Occupied by the ruler of Imperious.

Neither of us is surprised.

"Case," I say dryly.

She smiles evilly. "So, you survived! Oh, how wonderful."

"What are you doing?" I ask.

"Well, what do you think I'm doing, Love?" She says. "I am taking what is rightfully mine."

"That doesn't belong to you," Cos says. Case shoots a disapproving glance at Leader Hawse, caged with Demi. Cos turns to him.

"Is it true, Dad?"

"Oh, shame on you, Hawsey boy!" Case chimes in. "Keeping family from your own son?"

"Dad?" Cos says.

"Yes," Hawse speaks up now, "It's true. She's my twin. The aunt your brother went looking for. Did you find him?"

Cos shakes his head as Case taunts them. "Make that older twin sister," Case scowls.

"By seconds!" Hawse spits.

"And older all the same, Brother!"

"He's dead." Cos says and that draws back Hawse's attention.

"What?"

Cos just looks at him and then turns away. I speak up to draw the attention away from him.

"We know something else is going on here, Case. Why else are you here? What are they after?" As she answers, I notice a guard who appears to be hiding off to the side.

"Well, why do you think?" Case says.

"I don't know," I reply. "Why don't you tell me?"

"I, as I am sure you have come to realize, was born on Obsequious but never bought the servile attitude. At an early age, I knew I was destined for far greater things. But because of this darkening attitude, as they liked to call it, my rightful place as heir was given to my younger brother." She glares at him as she speaks. As she does, I try to get the guard's attention. It may be an ill attempt for escape, but he is already in hiding. So, I take a chance. Maybe this guard will have a change of heart and help me. It's our only option right now.

"I then ran away to an Imperious in ruins, usurped that throne and raised them to victory. It is because of that victory that I now stand here today, prepared to take over both kingdoms and rule them as one. Simple."

I subtly wave my hands behind my back and sporadically look over my shoulder. I am unable catch his full face, but he gets my message and stands. I motion to his sword and he nods from his hiding spot. I hide a smirk at having successfully devised some sort of plan, however untrustworthy, however risky, still a plan.

"The Colonel contacted me a few weeks ago, promising his help in exchange for my secret." Case finishes.

"Wait," I say. "Explained what?"

"Our cultural kisses…" She gives an odd grin at the words. "Our strength kisses."

"What?" As I speak, the guard holding me captive trades places with someone. I look to the other guard's hideout and notice that he is gone. He understood what I meant. He is going to help me to escape. I suppress a grin. I may actually be able to break myself out of this. I can still win.

"I want you to join me, Suudella. Come back to where you belong."

"You're sure you want that, Case? After all, I never was strong enough."

"And I'm offering you a truce. No hard feelings, a life time of luxury."

"You took my family from me," I spit. "My brother, my parents…"

She laughs obnoxiously. "Yes, indeed it was I that killed

your parents." I bite my tongue at the confirmation. "But I did it for your own good, child. And my own. They knew, you know. About all of this. They knew. And that just couldn't be."

I lash out then, attempt to break free and attack her.

"You evil, cunning, good-for-nothing bastard!" I scream. "Bring them back to me! Give them back!" The guards hold me back and I topple to my knees.

"They are dead, Suudella. They were dead from the day they handed you over to me." Her grin drips with evil. "Bring the Colonel," Case orders. "He might enjoy this as well." Three guards go to fetch him.

Cos still kneels bound by a guard, staring at the ground. He has given up.. The Colonel walks in from a door to the right with Lenten by his side. Case goes to greet them, brings them back to the throne.

I gather Cos' attention and nod to the guard behind me, try to silently explain my plan. He looks at the guard and the expression that spreads across his face is next to unreadable. He turns white, looks as if he has seen a ghost.

I frown, but I shake my head to prepare for my getaway, devising a way for me to get Cos out of this too.

I take a deep breath.

"Now!" I scream and my bondage is cut. I flick my wrists for my Veitsen and turn to Cos who shakes his head at me vigorously.

"What—"

"Not so fast, Hun." A gun clicks behind my head, but I am already frozen. I know that voice. "The party is just getting started," The playful tone. "Where ya headed, Love?" The audible smirk. He chuckles. That chuckle…

I slowly stand and turn to face the guard that holds me at gunpoint. I don't want to see, I don't want to see, I don't want to see…

"Hector," I say. My eyes are wide and moist.

"Did you miss me?" He asks. "'Cuz I sure missed you."

# CHAPTER 13

I have not moved from my kneeling position. It has merely been seconds since I saw Hectors all-knowing grin as he held a gun to my forehead.

He still holds it there.

I look up at him, almost begging him to pull the trigger. "You were…dead," I manage to say.

I was right. I was being plotted against. He did want to befriend me and then make me fall for him before he delivered the final blow. But he is not who I thought he was. It was Hector all along.

"Aw, Honey…did you really think I was so stupid as to not duck at gunfire?"

"I just…" He takes the gun away from my head and squats in front of me.

"I stood so I'd get shot in the chest. Case thinks we're

all dead and you and lover boy over there leave me behind. It was the perfect plan. You both performed perfectly." He stands again and I take a moment to look at Cos. He stares at Hector in disbelief. "I'm just thankful that all that talk about burning my body stayed as talk. Because that," he says, running his fingers gently over the pistol. "Would have ruined everything." He grins down at me again and I look away as I feel my heart being physically taken from within my chest. "And how did you morons not even notice how unusually buff I'd become in that vest and bags of cow blood? I mean, geez. Even I was a little skeptical of how believable it was." He continues grinning down at me. "But you just trusted me way too much, didn't ya, Del?"

I am empty. I can barely stand to look at him. It is too much to take in. I almost hate myself. "I trusted you…" My voice trails as emotions get the better of me.

"Yes, you did. And it worked out perfectly." He still smiles down at me and my sadness begins transforming into rage. Before I can even move in his direction, before I have a chance to lash out yet again, he moves swiftly to the side and walks away.

"Guards, will one of you please get that wretched woman off of my throne?" I glance at him for a second and then look away. The rage has faded. I am immobile. I do not know what to do.

The guards come and yank me to my feet. They drag me and Cos across the oversized room and into a hallway on the left. We pass by Demi and Leader Hawse on the way.

"You'll be okay, Del," says Demi. I simply nod.

"What is going on?" I hear Case yell from behind me. "Colonel, this is not what we discussed!"

"That you are right about," Hector says to Case. "You were the bait. And you had all the answers," he says. "But you are of no use now. "Execute her!"

The guards grab her and drag her towards me. I can tell because her voice becomes louder with ever step. They throw her in the cage with Hawse and Demi. And then it clicks.

My eyes widen as the door shuts.

They are all in the execution cage.

Case is going to die.

Hawse is going to die.

Demi is going to die.

And who knows?

I'll probably die too.

Cos and I sit in a prison.

I guess we were too much of a liability to throw in the execution cage.

Or maybe they don't want us dead yet.

They keep us separate. Cos stays at the far end of his cage and I stay on the far end of mine. Neither of us knows what to do with the other.

I just sit and stare at the rusting bars that I rest my head against.

I felt like maybe Cos and I could have made up a few hours ago. It'd seemed like he had let go of what had happened. But I know now he must blame me, must think this is my fault.

In many ways, it is. I was the one who trusted Hector, not him. He knew, he sensed it, but I ignored him. I'm not surprised he's angry with me.

I curl up into the corner and hug my knees then, feeling more alone than I've ever thought myself capable,

I should be the only person I need.

I always have been in the past.

But I can't be anymore.

Everything's changed down to the last bare necessity.

But I stay curled up there, saying a silent prayer that somehow God get me out of this.

Even though I know I do not deserve it.

I don't deserve anything.

"I'm still here," Cos says quietly.

I turn out of my corner enough to see him, still holding on to my knees, He has moved to the front of his cage, to the bars that join our cells.

"Are you?" I ask.

He just nods. "Yes."

We sit silently for a moment, still cautious, still shaken, still unsure of how to approach one another. And then, "Del."

"Yeah?"

"You said something the other day that I've been thinking about, something about your brother. I don't..." He trails. "I don't know if now is a good time, if there ever is one, but, we're probably going to be here a while and..." he sighs. "I don't know. I just—"

"He was my first kill."

"Oh."

I nod. "Yeah." The word comes out as a sigh, like I have breathed a part of me away. "It was in the training facility where your people attacked mine, the day we met." I begin. "The day I fought you, I had my mentee Demi, the little girl locked up with your father, do what we call a Center Mat fight. You screw up? Center Mat, you're instructor wants to see the best of you? Center Mat. Case wants to see you kill...Center Mat." I pause and bite into my lip. I can only breathe...

"Del," Cos whispers. "It's okay."

"So, I called Demi to fight a little boy that day for his punishment, because I knew she would win. The fight only stops when the instructor who called the fight says to stop."

"Did you?" Cos asks.

"Yes, but I probably should have called it a little sooner. I only stopped it because Lenten told me to. Otherwise..."

"She would have killed him?"

"Exactly." There is a short emptiness in the room as I hesitate.

"What happened Del?"

"Case called me into her office that day, angry with me for having Demi fight. She said my reasoning was too personal. I guess in the past few days I've realized she was right about one thing..." I take one more breath before diving in.

"When I was Demi's age, I was called to a Center Mat fight. But this one she called for in private because I was to be fighting my brother, Zed. She didn't want anyone to be too distracted by it, she said. So, she called us to the fight and I was naturally stronger, me being a year and a half older.

"I stopped on my own when he'd begun to stop squirming. And I looked into his hazel eyes and saw them pleading, I saw him begging for me to stop. So I did and I began to stand up and help him up off of the ground, knowing the rules, but also having morals.

"Naturally Case disapproved. She yelled at me, screamed at me. 'Keep going, Del. Keep going! Finish him!' But I was done. I couldn't kill my own brother! He was my brother. My own blood.

"And Case didn't like that. So, she walked onto the mat and spun me around. She spun me around slapped me, hard across the face. 'Be a ruler, Del. Be the princess I trained you to be! You're weak! Weak!' Then she slapped me again and I fell to the ground.

"All I remember is hearing the room go completely silent, muffled from the hit. And I remember looking behind me and seeing my brother's unmoving body on the ground." I pause for a long moment and take a deep breath. "She finished him for me." At that moment, Cos's face softens as he looks at me.

"Del, you didn't kill him."

I nod my head slowly. "Yes I did. I did. I could have hit her back, made her kill me instead or faked it with him so he could run away. I could have done anything. But I let her finish him. I knew what she was doing, knew what she would do. And I let it happen."

"It isn't your fault, Suudella. You can't blame yourself for this."

"I almost did it to somebody else!"

"Doesn't matter, Del. You didn't. And that's all that matters."

I nod. "Case is an evil, conniving genius." I say. "And she isn't even the mastermind behind all of this." Cos gives a soft chuckle at my semi joke. I get up and move to the other side of the cage so that the bars are the only things separating us from one another.

"Thank you," I say.

Cos looks at me and smiles. I feel his fingers as they lace through mine as all of our shared confusion dissipates and we finally see each other again. "You're welcome."

"Well, would you look at that!" Hector swaggers into the prison with two guards then. "They're holding hands, aw how sweet." He turns and whispers something to one of the guards.

The guard leaves and Hector is let into Cos' cage by the other. "Rise, loser." He smirks and Cos looks at him with a scowl. "I said get up, dark prince."

He kicks him and Cos clutches his side. After a second kick, he then throws a knife that scrapes his thigh.

"Stop it!" I scream. Hector looks at me and his grin widens.

"What? Oh! Am I hurting him?" He kicks Cos again and he lies on his side, clutching his bleeding thigh. By now I am standing and hopeless to help Cos. "Too bad."

Hector lifts him up by the collar and then punches him hard in the face. He then drops him back onto the ground.

"Your turn, Lovely." Hector leaves Cos cage and is then let into mine. I stand directly in the center of the cell, waiting. "Ah, you're ready for me. I like it!" He closes the cage door behind himself and stands in front of me. "Why don't I save you the pain and you just give me a kiss, eh?"

I stand unmoving, glaring at a face I once saw a friend in.

"No? Well, then I'll just have to take one." He grabs me at the waist and smacks his mouth into mine, but I kick him in the shin before it escalates. "Oh, so you want to play rough?"

I punch him across the face and prepare as he touches a hand to his bloody mouth and then looks up at me over his eyelids. "I can play rough, Honey. You don't want that."

In less than a moment, I am on the ground. There is a stinging sensation on my left cheek and a ringing in my left ear. He hit me so hard all I remember is falling to the ground. He then straddles me and squeezes my face in one hand.

"You were always, so beautiful," he says in a raspy whisper into my ear. My eyes water from the hatred coursing through my body, filling me from head to toe. So many missed cues, so many signs so clear that I ignored . And for what?

Imprisonment.

Separation.

And now this.

Violation.

He licks the side of my face as he straddles me. I don't fight back this time, hoping that takes the fun out of it for him. Instead, I just lay there as he sits on top me and let it be. Besides, anything I try to do will only tire me out and make matters worse.

Out of the corner of my eye, I can see Cos watching. I want so badly for him to reach through the bars and grab him, but he doesn't. He can't. Not if he wants to live. I don't blame him.

Just as Hector is about to continue harassing me, the guard that left returns with Lenten and Tessa. He calls to

Hector. "Sir, Hector. The Colonel would like to speak with you." He lets my face go and stands. "Tell him I'm on my way, will ya?"

He spits out his blood on me. He then leaves my cage and walks towards the exit. "Tessa," He says to her as he walks by. "My favorite Imperian traitor,"

"Yeah boss?" She looks at him with satisfaction.

He drapes his arm around her shoulders and leans down to her height. "Which one do you want, kiddo?"

"I'll take..." I already know she wants to kill me, but she draws it out like nothing I've ever seen. "I'll take the boy." She says and my heart falls flat. "You said she loves him, right?" Tessa and Hector both laugh and I can almost scream.

"That means, Colonel Jr.?" Hector looks to Lenten who directs his gaze away from me.

"Yeah?" I am taken by his lack of enthusiasm.

"You get Princess over there. Maybe you guys can catch up a bit? Reminisce..." He grins as he walks out to meet the Colonel and Tessa goes into Cos' cage. He sits up now and clutches his thigh. It is bleeding, but the knife barely scraped it, thankfully.

"Get up," Tessa demands. He looks up at her in pain.

"I can't...he stabbed my—" And he calls out in pain. I stifle a grin at his performance. Smart guy.

"Well, that foils the fun I had planned for us." Tessa sighs. "I swear he is so stupid sometimes...Guards! Carry him out." One of the guards immediately goes to grab Cos and Lenten nods for the other to go with them. Once they're gone, he enters my cage and sits at a friendly distance.

Lenten looks at me for a long moment as I right myself against the bars, wiping Hector's blood saliva mix off of me. He continues staring and it gets the better of me.

"What are you looking at?"

"I'm sorry," he says. I roll my eyes and wipe my mouth. I can still taste him…unpleasant.

"Of course you are."

"No, really. I didn't…" He leans forward then. "Del you have to believe me I didn't know about any of this. They weren't supposed to…" He sighs. I don't respond. "My Dad… he's been observing you guys for years."

"What does that even mean?" I'm not even sure I want to know.

"He works for the government. They're mostly interested in 'Expansion.' Colonizers have been doing it for millenniums. But a few years ago they received word from a soldier that he and his crew had witnessed something really…unusual down in what used to be the USA."

"What are you talking about? What is that?"

He shakes his head and almost laughs. "You know, when I moved to Imperious to start the mission all those months ago, I'd heard that a lot of the history had been lost, but it wasn't until I actually got there, in the heat of it, that I realized how much was actually gone. You've lost it all." He says.

"Lost what?" I am almost yelling from the frustration.

"Some century or two ago the world split."

"Yes, I know. Into two halves."

He shakes his head. "That's what you all are taught down here. But actually of the continents split. North America, where you and I are from, split into five. I'm from the top portion."

"What's it called?"

"Canada." I frown. He laughs. "As far as I know, we're the only country left that still uses its name from antiquity. And when our colonizers rediscovered this land, where you live, where we are now, they were ecstatic, but also alarmed. Because there was a war going on down there and the people had practices they'd never seen.

"He sent me down for the primary investigation, inserting myself seamlessly into society to observe. Nothing turned up though, so he went on to phase two. The only way he could get that going was with more funding from the Prime Minister, disguising the mission with expansion as the primary goal. And everything worked out fine until the Prime Minister's son demanded full leadership of the exploration."

"Thus, Hector,"

"Precisely."

"Why are you telling me all of this?" I ask. I can barely wrap my brain around it.

"So you can understand. You were never supposed to be apart of this. I made them promise to leave you out of it. But Tessa..." I look away. "And, maybe, I'm just doing this for my on conscience, but I also think you might be able to figure out a way out of this." I still don't look at him or respond. "Look, Del, Case was just bait, a cover, and a way in. My dad is here for science. The Liables are just extra strength on their side. But Hector? Hector wants to wipe out all of your people and Cos' just for the sake of owning more land." We lock eyes. "We have to stop him."

"But what can we do, we don't have anything to use against him."

"I know. Except maybe the kiss." He says.

"What?"

"What the soldier saw, what my dad his been studying, Case mentioned it earlier too. It's the energy exchange that occurs between Imperians and their victims. It's what She's been hiding for decades, it's what she killed your parents over…we can use that against him." He pauses. "Somehow." As he speaks, I remember the battle on the beach and the heaving chests I noticed in the dead Obsequains.

"But how? How is that an advantage?"

"He doesn't know about it. For him, this is all about expansion…" he trails off. "And it might not be. But it's all we've got."

"Why are you helping me?"

He just shrugs. "It's the right thing to do. And I feel like I owe it to your people. In many ways, I am a traitor too. For that, I am sorry."

I sit and stare at the ground. I can barely move, barely think. Everything is scrambling around in my head, swimming in my own thoughts. This is all too much.

"I'm also glad you found Cos," He says after a moment. "Maybe the legend really will find its way to fruition…"

Just then the door slams open enters and Lenten immediately takes a sword from his belt and holds it at me.

"Glare at me one more time and I swear—"

"Lenten. Let's go." It's the Colonel.

"Okay, Dad," He says. He turns to face me as he puts the sword back in his belt. He looks me in the eyes and smiles.

"Remember the kiss. It's all you've got against him." He whispers. And then he smiles gently before walking toward his father who makes his way to the exit.

"Wait," Lenten says. "What about Tessa?" he gestures to the direction that she took Cos in.

"We are leaving," The Colonel says. "She can stay here."

"But Dad—"

"That is it, Lenten! We are leaving." And he walks stiffly through the exit. Lenten gives me another tight smile before following closely behind.

And thus I am left in my prison cage alone, waiting for Cos' return and fearing that Hector may.

# CHAPTER 14

I awake to a kiss on my forehead.

At first I let it happen, but then I think of all the possibilities of who it could be and sit up abruptly.

"Relax," Cos says. "It's only me," I open my eyes completely and look at him astonished that he is still in one piece.

"Cos," I say and throw myself into his arms without hesitation. He hugs me back and we sit on the ground holding on to one another. "I'm so sorry for everything. It's my fault we're in this. If I hadn't been so quick to trust Hector and not you…"

"I know," he says pulling away and looking down at me. "I'm sorry too."

I let a small smile form as I hug him again but pull away quickly upon realization. "Wait. How did you get in my cage?"

"Tessa kind of made me a promise," he says with a small smirk.

"What did she do to you?" I say, looking him up and down.

"Not what you're thinking, now relax. We can figure this all out together now. We only have one cage to worry about." He says with a chuckle. He rubs my back with his hand and I feel more secure than I ever have in my life.

"Thank you," I say and he keeps smiling.

"You're welcome," He says softly and then plants another kiss on my forehead. I lean into him again and sigh. "So, what are we going to do?" He asks.

"I don't know, but Lenten gave me a lot of good information. And I've been thinking about it all night. I may know how to defeat Hector and save our countries from the expansion."

"Save our...what?"

"Long story. Just—"

"Okay, so I hate to break up this love fest, but I have about thirty seconds to break you guys out of here, so let's cooperate, shall we?"

I break away from Cos' grasp and crawl over to the cage entrance. "Lenten? I thought you left."

"Yeah, well I convinced my father to stay the rest of the night so I could sneak out, as I have, and set you guys free." He unlocks the gate.

"Well, what did you tell him?" Cos walks out the gate but I stay by the entrance with Lenten.

"I told him I wanted to say goodbye to Tessa." the grin on his face is so wide I can't help but smile myself. Before I take off, I embrace him. "and for the record, I never liked her." I give a small laugh.

"Thank you, Lenten. For everything." And then I kiss him on the cheek. He blushes a little.

"Of course. Did you figure something out?"

"Maybe. It's a long shot, but it just might work." I say with a nod.

"Then go! Get out of here and good luck!" He pushes me off toward Cos and we grab hands and run past the main exit and to the window on the side.

"This is probably our best bet," Cos says as he opens it. He boosts me through and I hop down to the ground, thankful that it wasn't several stories high. He hops down beside me, taking my hand again, and we run back around to the main entrance of the palace.

"Are we going in the same way as last time?" Cos asks over the wind.

"Absolutely," I say and we burst through the doors of the palace once again.


"Oh, so happy you could join us," Hector says when we enter. "We have been waiting for you guys." I scowl at his tone of voice. Everything is a game with him. Now the party can begin." He sighs. "I always knew there was a traitor in our midst."

"Party's over, Hector. It's time to end this." I say.

"Oh, my queen. Be my queen, will ya, Del?" He picks up a rose out of a nearby planter and holds it to his nose as he makes his way over to me. "Be my beautiful, queen…" I clench my jaw at the thought and he tosses the rose in my face with a roaring laugh. "Say yes and I'll let you live," He teases, his breath hot on my face.

"What about Cos?" I say, humoring him.

"Oh, him? I was never going to let him live," And then he rips out his sword and thrusts it at Cos. Cos, with his superior training, dodges it easily and manages to take it away.

Hector roars with anger now as he takes a sword from one of his many guards and approaches him again. Cos looks at me and uses his eyes to point towards the gate that holds Case, Hawse, and Demi. I give a slight nod and slowly make my way over as Cos and Hector battle.

I make it to the cage but there is only a second before Tessa attacks me. "It can't be that easy, right?" She says as she lunges at me with a sword.

"Can you even use that thing, Tess?"

"Of course," she says with a lack of confidence. I suppress a smirk. I dodge several swipes with ease when I notice Demi motioning for my attention.

When I look at her, my heart aches seeing her locked in a cage. I feel as though I have failed her. It's my job as coming leader of Imperious to protect my people, especially the young children. And yet here she stands, like a caged animal.

She continues motioning at something. I frown, unable to understand what she is trying to tell me at first, but she points behind me. I spin around and notice Lenten in the exit from the prison. He holds two small knives in his hand, a small smirk on his face.

I kick the sword out of Tessa's hand effortlessly and she screams as she goes to retrieve it. I turn and run quickly, taking the gift from Lenten and returning his engaging smile.

"Forgot to give you these on your way out," he says. And then he whispers, "Go, get her." I almost laugh.

I ready myself and then charge at my enemy for the first time without the intention of killing them. Fighting a female is indeed different, but if I could do it once, I can easily do it again.

She takes swipes at me repeatedly with that oversized sword of hers, but she cannot manage to hit me. She can barely maneuver with it, struggling to hold it up, struggling to swing. I was always better than her, but the fact that she is using someone else's weapon makes it all the easier.

She leaps at me and I duck without a thought, causing her to land on herself. To her luck, she did not stab herself in the process, but she does fall hard so it will take her a minute to get up.

I run over to the cage and pick the lock with my knife, a skill I perfected years ago. Once open, Demi and Hawse run into the prison hall to hide. Demi stops at the entrance before turning around and running to me. She jumps into my arms.

"Thank you, Del," she says and I nod my head. Any words I should try to speak would come out in a sob. She jumps down and runs back to Hawse safely as the aching in my heart slowly subsides.

I turn to the cage again and notice Case has remained inside. I point my knife at her. "If you move, I will kill—" I stop myself short. No, I think. No more killing, no more slaughter.

"I will imprison you myself." I correct. She cowers into her corner and I walk out to see Tessa charging at me yet again, sword above head. I simply side step out of the cage and she trips and finds herself inside with a possibly broken ankle. I stifle a laugh at how amusing this so-called battle has been. It was more like practice as opposed to life or death.

With her taken care of, I look to Hector and Cos who are in a pretty even fight. Both have given up on the swords, too big for even them to handle. As the fight progresses, I realize that our only chance for things to settle down is to get Hector into the cage with Tessa and Case. If we can do that, we'll stand a chance against the rest.

"Cos!" I call out. I have placed myself directly in front of the cage doorway so he sees it.

"What?" He calls. He hasn't yet looked. Why hasn't he looked?

"Cos!" I repeat. "I'm over here!" He finally glances and I watch the serious and concentrated look in his eyes fade as he realizes how simple his fight has become.

"Don't worry!" He calls. "I'm coming!"

Hector is oblivious to the entire situation, putting all his energy into keeping up with Cos. Cos continues walking backward, slowly, one step at a time. But when finally he is near the cage, Hector catches on, turning sharply and kicking Cos so he stumbles inside the cage instead. As he lies on the ground, in too much pain to move, he just nods. With that, I know exactly what he is telling me to do.

I have to lock him inside with Tessa.

And then fight Hector myself.

Just then, arms wrap around my neck. I kick the gate shut

and slip over the attacker, landing on my hands and feet, he landing on his back.

"You idiots really thought that would work?" He asks from the ground, rolling over.

"There's no way I'm letting you be my last kiss," I say, getting up off of the ground. He hops up and spits blood out of his mouth.

"What does that mean? Still got a little crush on me?"

"You wish," I spit and he charges for me, sending a left hook that I dodge. I sweep my foot under his legs, and he stumbles but doesn't fall. I give a round-house kick that he dodges easily, grabbing my foot and sending me spinning to the ground. I am taken by his almost superior combat skills.

"Now," he straddles me and grabs hold of my face with one hand. "What were you saying about that kiss everyone keeps talking about?" He leans down, breathing heavily onto me.

"I wouldn't tell you if it killed me."

"Maybe so. But he might." And then he looks up at Cos, locked in the cage, held in an unfortunate headlock by Tessa. That must have been some fall he took. "Hey, Lover Boy. Tell me about this secret kiss and I'll let her live." Tessa gives him another squeeze and he squirms. Now is our only chance. Hector doesn't know. If we act now then maybe we really can use it against him. "Tell you what," Hector continues. "I hate being out of the loop so much, I'll throw your life in too. And your dad's. For safe measure." Cos squirms some more.

"Just tell him, Cos," I say, attempting to seize the moment. "Tell him the truth. About how we kiss our victims before we kill them. To show compassion."

"Oh, is that so?" He leans down again and looks at me. "I surely like the sound of that. With you, at least."

"No! It's—" Tessa tries. Cos finally gathers the strength and momentum to fight back then, turning things around and choking the voice out of her.

"What was she going to say, Del?" Hector pesters. Tessa continues trying to speak, but Cos has her mouth covered and body wrapped. I don't speak. He squeezes my jaw harder than before and I whimper in pain.

"It's not for compassion." I manage. He begins to smile. "It gives us strength. A kiss before a kill creates an energy exchange. Every time." And suddenly the most sinister of smiles hovers before me.

"Perfect," is all he says. And he presses his mouth aggressively into mine. As he does, I manage to get one hand free and feel for my Veitsen. When it is within my grasp, with all the strength I can muster, I bite down on his tongue just seconds before thrusting my knife into his abdomen. He pulls up, his face stricken, before rolling over onto the floor. I stand and grab him by his collar.

"Of course, if you knew anything about anyone besides yourself or listened even a little bit you'd have known we kiss our victims after the kill." His face is still awestruck. "But even you aren't worth that." And I let him go, writhing and bloody on the glossy floor.


But it's not over. Before I have a moment to think, Liables come in a barrage at that moment, seeing their wounded leader and attacking. I fight back to the best of my superior abilities, but I am greatly outnumbered.

"Cos!"

"Del, listen!"

"What?"

"Listen,"

"I can't! You need to—"

"Just. Listen."

"Okay wait!" I put up my hands in surrender and the Liables stop, confusion on their filthy faces. The Obsequian guards are still unmoved. "Shh," I say quietly. "Listen," Everyone in the room begins looking around, eyes searching for what the ears need, mind searching for what only one of us has heard. And then we hear it. Everyone's eyes widen as the sound grows. Outside, through the door…Cos, Del, Cos, Del, Cos, Del, Cozdel, Cozdel, Cozdel…over and over again.

I turn to Cos, still locked in the cage. "Do you think—" I begin.

He nods. "Yes," Cos says gently, cutting me off. And then he looks down at me with silvery eyes. "They came."


In seconds, Obsequians and Imperians charge in as one. I break Cos out of his cage first chance I get and we watch intently as our kingdoms work together to fight against the Liables and the Obsequian guards who decided to stay on Hector's side.

It is one of the most amazing sights I have ever seen, a rainbow of colors, accented by the same shade of black. Men and women helping one another, rolling over backs, flipping into Liables backing each other up against guards with heavy swords that even they have trouble managing. Even Lenten joins the fight, defending anyone he can against the Liables. It is something that I never thought I would see, and something I never thought I would want to. But this moment, I realize is a moment I have subconsciously been waiting for my entire life. And here it is.

Together.

The fighting goes on for what feels like hours, but it's really only a matter of minutes. Bodies falling here and there but Imperians and Obsequians working as a team, as one country, as one body of people.

But this isn't over yet. Hector still has more people on his side, the government from the other place Lenten was talking about. I have to find the right way, the right words, the right time…There is no need for me to join in. It's time for me to lead, for both of us, Cos and me to stand up for our homes.

So, I find my feet walking, taking me over to the throne where Case sat before. I stand on the platform above it and watch, breathe in the newfound trust that has become of these two rivaling countries. This, the unified fight against a greater cause, is exactly what the world needed, this is exactly the change that needed to occur.

And I need to gather everyone's attention.

Because there is no longer a reason for a war to go on. There is no need for battle. The Imperians and Obsequians now get along as one, and Liables no longer have to isolate themselves from the war because there isn't one.

There is no war to be in.

We can all live together in unison.

I gather myself, brush the dirt and filth off of my clothes and almost smile. I almost smile because things can change, the world can change, we can all change! It isn't just me. We all need this. And here it is. This is it.

Because together we can stop the expanders.

But then a number of events take place, and I forget what I had planned, forget what I ever wanted to say or why or how or when…

I become a random Imperian girl standing on a royal platform as Hector manages to stand despite his wounds and finds a gun lying on the ground.

And then he screams as he points it at Cos and pulls the trigger.

But Lenten, watching the entire situation, runs.

And he runs.

And he runs…

Until he is with in range and he pushes…he pushes Cos out of the way.

Everything stops.

The gun fire rings throughout the palace.

All fighting ceases.

All heads turn.

The resonating gunfire stops the room cold.

I see the Colonel as he watches from afar.

He falls to his knees, unable to bear it.

Cos sees my stricken expression from the ground he landed on.

And he watches me, I know he does, I know it. I can feel it.

But I do not see Cos.

Because all I see is Lenten, the boy I loved in the beginning, the one who understood in the end. A lover, a teacher, and a friend.

All I see is his dying body on the ground.

Tessa screams from her caged space.

Hector ignores the silence and his own spilling blood as he wipes his mouth on the collar of his shirt. Satisfied. I do not stop him as he limps out of the palace.

I can't.

Instead I just run.

I run with everything I can to Lenten.

I have to say goodbye. He can't die without anybody saying goodbye, he can't close his eyes and merely see the lights above.

He needs to see a friendly face.

And I make it just in time.

I grab him and wrap him in my arms, pull him onto my lap and rest his head against me.

"Hey, hey," I say through falling tears. "Everything is going to be okay. You are going to be okay, I promise. Life isn't letting go of you yet."

"Suudella?" He struggles to speak. He has two shots to the chest and one to the stomach. I'm surprised he is even still breathing. But I am glad he is. "Suudella," He whispers my full name and I feel worse, I feel at fault even though I know I am not. "Thank you, thank you…so much." He struggles. "You…you changed…you…"

He looks into my eyes and reaches a hand up to my face,

brushes his fingertips against my cheeks. "You changed..." he repeats. His tone is happy, is forgiving, it's as if his only true desire was to see me become a real person. He spoke of my world having been unknowing. Maybe in moving here, in getting to know me, maybe that did become one of his deepest desires. Maybe he wasn't the person I knew him as after all.

He was different. He saved Cos and me. He was. He is. He always will be.

Cos comes up beside me, puts an arm around my waist and uses the other to brush Lenten's hair off his face.

"Hey, buddy," Cos is near tears. They did not know one another, but reguardless of country of origin, everyone knows that sacrifice is the upmost form of respect and honor. Cos is only still alive because of Lenten's sacrifice. He knows it. Everyone around still watches intently. The pinnacle of battle. The pinnacle of the war. "You, you saved me..."

"She needs you," Lenten says. "They need you..." "They need you. Cos, Del." He whispers.

And he doesn't breathe again.


After a matter of minutes I stand. I stand and grab Cos' hand and pull him up with me. And then he follows me to the platform where I stood before.

Everyone's gaze follows us. They follow him and they follow me and they follow our laced fingers. Nobody disapproves. Nobody speaks out against it.

"This is the result of war." I say. I stand tall and I hold my head high, letting the words sink in. I want them to feel it, to feel how I feel.

I want them to understand.

This is all our doing.

From past to future, we've stayed the same.

And that just can't be.

"This is the result of centuries of hatred." I continue. "Because one of us didn't die, no. The boy who has been here for merely months is the one who has been killed. The boy away from home. The boy of innocence." I pause again and watch the shifting movements, the fluttering eyes, the few tears that fall.

"This is all our fault. We have been fighting for centuries on end, for no real reason. Because we like power, because we like bloodshed, because we bathe in the pain of others.

"But this must end. We have to change it. And we have to change it now. Because if we don't, we will lose our land, our countries, ourselves. There is another war coming. And it is time, friends."

Cos continues from where I stop.

"We have to do this together, Obsequian, Imperian, and Liable, together, we must teach of confidence and selflessness and share in our experiences so we may fight to continue to exist. Together, we can save our countries and in their place build a new one, a place, a home for all of us to share with every ounce of happiness we can muster."

"Together," I say.

"Together," Cos repeats.

Then we hold our intertwined hands up and everyone in the room, in unison, "Together."

# EPILOGUE

A year ago, I would have never expected this to happen.

A year ago, I would never have even fathomed such an idea.

But, a year ago, I was an entirely different person.

After everyone actually agreed to unify, Tessa and Case were imprisoned. They both accepted it graciously and have received decent treatment based on their change in behavior. I visit every now and then to show them my forgiveness, and to let them know that I really have changed and that change is often times a very good thing.

Demi returned to her home with her parents and is growing up to be the lovely girl that she is. I also publicly announced a few months prior to now that she would be my successor should it be necessary, for I have no other family.

Lenten was given a beautiful Imperian funeral in Obsequious just before his father returned home with his remains.

Hector was never found. His absence only furthers our suspicions. There is a war coming. But now, as one country, one kingdom, we just might be able to put up a fight. We still may have an upper hand, so long as the Colonel never shares his research.

We have made contacts with other countries that still exist to this day and through them have learned about our own true history, the history of the United States and the rest of North America. In light of this, we have implemented a new governmental system that may aid us in our fight for victory.

Because the fight will come. But we will be ready, just as we always have been.

It is only now that I think about how well everything has turned out for us. Us being Cos and me. Because I stand in front of a full-length mirror in a long, off-white coronation dress.

Cos and I decided to rule together whilst implementing a more inclusive government. So, here I am, eighteen years old preparing to put a crown on my head, something I have dreamed of for years in a very different way. This I never saw in my future. But it is happening and I cannot contain my utter joy.

I smile at myself in the mirror, proud of the woman I have become. It is only a moment before I notice the man dressed in white in the corner of my mirror, watching me.

I try to hide my surprise.

"Hello," I say politely. "How may I help you?" the man steps into the room with his hand outstretched. I turn to face him and meet him halfway, shaking it. I realize after a moment that he is the man I saw at the beach battle some months ago, and the only unanswered question to the puzzle that has become my life.

"I am Ezra," He says, giving my hand a gentle shake. He wears a small smile on his face. He is older, but you can see that he must have been very handsome in his day. And there is a slight familiarity that I cannot place, something that reminds me of someone else.

"It's very nice to meet you, Ezra. May I help you with something?"

"Actually, Sweetheart, I'd like to help you."

"I beg your pardon?"

"Sit down, please." He takes a seat on the nearby sofa, resting his hands on the cane he carries with him.

"Sir, I don't have time. You see, I am about to be coronated—"

"And I surely know it." He says. "You're being crowned beside my grandson."

I freeze in place. I feel as though I am looking at a ghost. Cos told me last year that his grandfather died. And yet here he sits. "But how?"

"Ah, I faked my death for the good of your co-king." The joking way in which he says it throws me almost literally off balance. He seems so passive about it, so accepting and almost happy that he let his family and friends believe that he had died.

"I do not understand…" I say slowly, my voice trailing at such confusion. "Why would you—"

"Would you like to learn about the Cozdle legend?" He

jumps in, cutting me off. "Would you like to learn where it comes from?"

I take a seat on the sofa beside him. "I figured I ought to share with you the truth since you both have been so successful." As he speaks, I get a good look at his face and realize what was always so familiar about it.

He looks like Cos. Like an older and much wiser version, but still Cos. His sharp features and the way the ends of his mouth turn down. He has a face that appears to be in deep thought, even when smiling. Just like Cos. And his eyes...the same shimmering green. He notices me watching and gives a small smile before turning his body so that is faces me. Ezra clears his throat and looks at me for a moment before diving into his story.

"I made it up," and he waits for me to respond. I don't. I just sit and wait for him to continue. "I made it up, devised it myself upon finding out that the non-biological princess of Imperious was the same age as my grandson, the Prince of Obsequious. I decided it was the perfect way to bring the warring countries together, uniting them with a story." He smiles for a second before continuing. "So, I learned all about you, and came up with that poem based on your personality versus his. Then I 'died' and went traveling, spreading the story to Liables everywhere in hopes that you would hear it. I gave it to him and told him to find you. It taught him how to be a man, and to stand for what he believed in."

He looks away at something in the far end of the room, some undefined object that causes him to squint and tilt his head to the side. Then he turns his gaze to me once again.

"And it taught you how to change and how to trust." He pauses once more and places a hand on mine. "To be the person God needs you to be." Ezra looks at me intently for a long moment, his eyes searching all about my face. "Do you believe you are doing the right thing?"

And then I return his stare, thinking. Everything I have done in the past few months has been for the good of my people, deriving my strength from them and prayer. So, I reply, "I do indeed. " And it is the truth.

"You are a good girl, Suudella. I am proud of you."

"Thank you, Sir. But I have to ask, does Cos know you're..."

"Alive?" I nod and he chuckles to himself as he stands. "Why yes indeed, child. He invited me!"

"Well, why did you fake your death? He loved—loves— you so much...Why would you do that?"

"He needed the motivation," And that is all he says. No further explanation.

He gives a small smile and looks off into some distant area in front of him. "I suppose I should also tell you that I was the person calling him when you all were hiding out in my old cabin. And the only person worth "finishing" was Case. Never you."

I am standing now and I give a tiny gasp. "That was you." He nods his head and looks to me again.

"Indeed it was." Then he turns slowly and readies himself to walk out of the door to the room. "Well, I'm going to leave you to it. You, Child, have a coronation to get to." And he gives me a warm smile before slowly walking out of the room. "I just want you to know, that I, along with many others in this new found world you have created, admire you and everything you have gone through. Everything you stand for and everything that you are is what we believe in. You, Suudella...Del...You have become our hope." And with that, with those final words, he leaves the room almost as silently as he entered.

I return to the mirror, in deep thought. I just met the real master mind, the genius behind the Cozdle, the man I owe my newfound life to. I would never have become who I am today if it had not been for that man and his sole dream of changing the world. He may admire me, but I will forever admire him.

I continue primping myself for the biggest day of my life, in front of the entire country as well as those from others who would like to attend. It is a big event if I may say so myself, larger than any other in our growing history. And I get to be a part of it, with Cos...we get to be the center of it. There is no greater honor. I fix my hair and prepare to walk out when a knock comes at my door.

It's Cos.

I smile at the sight of him in his tuxedo and he comes into the room.

"You look...beautiful," he says, astonished by my outer appearance.

"And you, Sir, look very handsome." I smile and he takes my hands in his.

"You ready for this?" We both look at our reflections in the mirror.

"Yeah," I respond, the nerves have finally hit me as I fully realize just how many people will be here, and how many people will watch this take place. It is the beginning of our history, it is the beginning of our change.

"It's a big day," he says, completing my thoughts. And then he looks at me.

"It is," I say.

"The day my dad passes his crown to me, and Case passes hers to you." He pauses and turns my face to look at his. "And the day we join our separate worlds as one body."

"It's time," I say with a smile. He lets out a deep breath and then pulls me with him towards the door. "This is it."

Once we enter the ceremony, hand in hand, it goes by quickly.

He gets his crown, passed from the hands of his father to him.

I get my crown, passed from the hands of Case to me.

And then, to my surprise, his grandfather coronates us.

He pledges to rule for one body of people as do I.

And we lace fingers in unity for the whole world to see. We show the world with that one embrace that we are now one unit, one person, one country, alive and thriving. Together.

We face the crowd, laced fingers in the sky, showing the world that our love for them and each other reigns over everything beneath God's sky. Everything is finally changing for the better and our world can finally grow upon itself, upon the unity, and upon this. A new Antiquity will be born, starting with this ceremony, this day, this moment, right here, right now.

But the only part I care to remember is at the end when he looks at me in the eyes with more emotion than I have ever seen in a man. He looks at me and I can see everything, his past, his future, but more than anything I can see the present. I can see how much he cares about me, Suudella Iza Calhoun in his special way.

And I can feel it in myself too. Never have I ever been happier, never have I ever looked at someone and truly felt good about who I have become. But that has now changed, because I am looking at this young man, Coz Lane Tempest in full, but my Cos...just Cos. I am looking at him right now and feeling every emotion any person has ever desired. I am looking at him and remembering who I was, accepting who I am now, and shaping who I am destined to become with him by my side.

"I do love you," he says gently. I look at him for a moment and remember the first time I saw him, all the feelings that had begun to brew instantaneously. None of that has changed.

"I know," I reply just as softly.

And it is in that moment that I realize that if it weren't him, nothing would have changed.

And if it weren't for change, this world would remain and empty place.

We were just two teenagers stuck in a horrible world still in the midst of a war, but we found a way, a new path...we changed what had been decided for us, we shifted our own fates, not only because of a few written words, but because of who we were and who we are and who we are slowly becoming. Day by day, changes are made, but one thing will forever remain the same.

He is Cos.

I am Del.

And together we became the legend, we are the legend, that shaped and changed the world.

Made in the USA
San Bernardino, CA
31 August 2017